1. 00

THREE ROTTEN EGGS

The Hamlet Chronicles
so far:

THREE
ROTTEN
EGGS

by Gregory Maguire

Illustrated by Elaine Clayton

Clarion Books / New York

This book is for Bill Reiss,
who helps to hatch only the best.

Clarion Books
a Houghton Mifflin Company imprint
215 Park Avenue South, New York, NY 10003
Text copyright © 2002 by Gregory Maguire
Illustrations copyright © 2002 by Elaine Clayton

The type was set in 12-point Baskerville Book.
The illustrations were executed in ink and ink wash.

Printed in U.S.A.

Library of Congress Cataloging-in-Publication Data

Maguire, Gregory.
Three rotten eggs / by Gregory Maguire ; illustrations by Elaine Clayton.
p.   cm.
"Volume 5 of the Hamlet chronicles."
Summary: The students of Miss Earth's class in rural Vermont experience
an eventful spring when they become involved with a bullying new student,
a competitive egg hunt, and genetically altered chicks.
ISBN 0-618-09655-8
[1. Schools–Fiction. 2. Eggs–Fiction. 3. Bullies–Fiction. 4. Spring–Fiction.
5. Vermont–Fiction. 6. Humorous stories.] I. Clayton, Elaine, ill. II. Title.
PZ7.M2762 Th 2002
[Fic]–dc21
2001047129

QUM   10 9 8 7 6 5 4 3 2 1

Humbody Dumbody sat on a wall.
Humbody Dumbody had a great fall.
Somebody ought to have told him that balance
Is one of the more indispensable talents.

CONTENTS

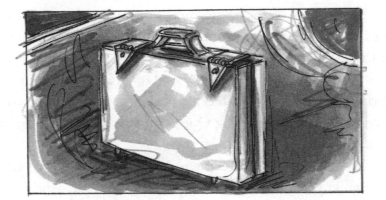

1. Highway Robbery

"Those clouds look positively packed with lightning," said Miss Earth to her students. "Inside, class. On the double."

The children were tying plastic Easter eggs onto a forsythia bush by their classroom window. But the sudden clouds did have a close, *gonna-getcha* feel to them. With unusual briskness, Miss Earth's students obeyed their leader and tumbled into the classroom.

Miss Earth went immediately to the radio to see if there was an emergency storm watch. The radio screeched with static. Then it settled and picked up a country-western song. The new hit by Petunia Whiner, Miss Earth's favorite singer. The teacher waited for the song to end, hoping for a weather update.

> *"Ya got a little baby and ya gotta treat it right.*
> *Ya gotta rock the cradle so your baby sleeps tight.*
> *Baby needs a diaper change, Baby has a poo.*
> *If Baby wakes and burps a lot, whatcha gonna do?*
> *Just cuddle cuddle cuddle till the cows come home."*

In a corner of the room, under cover of the sound of music, two girls resumed the argument they'd been having at the egg bush.

"I *never* get to be in charge!" said one. "Thekla Mustard, spring has arrived. It's time for a change. Why don't you take a vacation from being Queen Bee all the time? That'd be a *big* change."

"Lois," said the other, "face it. You're not me. You're nice enough in your own drab way, but you're not me. And I am the one who annually gets elected Empress. So if we girls are going to form a classroom girls' team at the annual Spring Egg Hunt, I get to govern it as I govern everything. With surprising mastery."

"You're such a power hog. I'd hate to see what you're going to be like when you grow up. Some crazy dictator."

"We'll see," said Thekla. "It's always an option."

"Girls," said their teacher. "Shh! Here comes the weather."

Thekla simpered. Lois frowned. There had to be some way to unseat the bossy Empress. Sooner or later Lois would find out how.

Vermont State Trooper Hiram Crawdad wheeled his cruiser around the cloverleaf linking Interstate highways 89 and 91. He was listening to the latest Petunia Whiner hit on Vermont Country Radio. Her whiskey-raw voice seemed like a soundtrack to a made-for-TV movie. Starring himself, of course. Tapping the time on his steering wheel, he listened and sang along.

> *"Ya got a little baby and ya gotta treat it right.*
> *Ya gotta kiss your baby and teach it not to bite.*

Baby starts to cry a little, Baby cries a lot.
Ya gonna throw the baby in the garbage? Not.
Just cuddle cuddle cuddle till the cows come home."

Trooper Crawdad was just emerging from the curve when he saw a snazzy orange coupe roaring along from the direction of New Hampshire. Doing eighty-five miles an hour, easy. "How-de-do, what's your hurry?" said the trooper. "You've just netted yourself a hefty fine, stranger. Welcome to Vermont." He accelerated as he left the interchange.

The deejay cut in. "That was Petunia Whiner in her hit single 'Baby Needs Burping.' Now a weather update from WAAK, the Voice of Vermont. Severe thunderstorm alert for the Upper Valley. Could change to snow—who knows. Spring is fickle around here."

The trooper turned off WAAK and hit the switch on his flashing blue and white lights. Best part of his job: sound, light, speed! And the mighty force of the law. The coupe came roughly to a halt in the melting slush at the side of the highway.

The trooper drew a breath and went to deal with the situation.

The driver bounded out of his car. He was a thin man in a pinstriped shirt. He was so angry that his face was flushing patriotically, red, white, and nearly blue. Even his mustache looked alert and trembling. "What'd you stop *me* for? I'm not the thief. Aren't you going to go after the motorcycle, you cretin?"

"Calling a state trooper a cretin is, well, a bit rude," said Trooper Crawdad. "If you don't mind, I'll ask the questions. Is there a good reason you are driving above the speed limit, sir? Especially when it looks like rain?"

As the trooper spoke, the storm shadows darkened the woods and fields on either side of the highway.

"I've been robbed!" cried the man. "I stopped to use the men's room in a McDonald's in West Lebanon, and a motorcyclist smashed the lock on my trunk and stole my briefcase!" He led the trooper around to the back of his car. Sure enough, the lock was smashed. "I was gaining on the motorcyclist when he lit off cross-country! I couldn't follow him, so I was hurrying to the next exit."

"I'll alert the local authorities, sir. License, please."

The man flipped his license at Trooper Crawdad and kicked a melting snow bank.

"Let's see. Professor Wolfgang Einfinger. What exactly did the fellow steal?" said Trooper Crawdad. "Didn't catch that part, Professor."

"My briefcase," said Einfinger. "That's all you need to know. And you better find it. The security of our nation just might depend on it."

"Oh, is that so?" said Trooper Crawdad.

But Einfinger clammed up. He wouldn't utter another word.

All over the town of Hamlet, Vermont, folks unplugged their computers and television sets. At his farm, Old Man Fingerpie unhooked his cows from the electric milking machine. No sense risking fried udders.

Grandma Earth, the local baker and auto mechanic, as well as Miss Earth's mother, ran outside to haul some fifty-pound sacks of flour from her pickup truck before they got soaked.

The first selectman of Hamlet, Mayor Timothy Grass,

was driving the street cleaner back to the town garage. He noticed a sleek black town car with tinted windows purring around the village green. "It rains on the rich and the poor alike," he said to himself.

In Clumpett's General Store, Olympia Clumpett was pouring coffee into a paper cup for a customer when the thunder finally let loose. The monstrous noise startled her. Lightning flashed at the same instant. The cloud must be directly overhead, she thought. For a moment, everything in the store seemed outlined in green neon. There was a malevolent smell of something sulfurous and scorched. A lightning strike? The church steeple? The white pines out back? "And us with one of our fire engines out of commission!" said Olympia. "Ooops. Sorry about that, fella." The coffee had gone all over the counter, and she had to get the customer a new cup.

"Weird weather for this time of year," said the customer. "Thunder in March?"

"It happens," said Olympia Clumpett, "but not often. And rarely so loud. That'll be a dollar even."

"Hey, Limpy," called her husband, Bucky, from the back room. "I hope you haven't got a customer there who parked a motorcycle out back?"

Olympia said, "By the look on his face, I think I do."

"At least," Bucky went on, "I *think* it was a motorcycle."

Olympia punched the stiff old keys on the antique cash register and said, "Sounds like your motorcycle just exploded. Milk and sugar with your coffee?"

2. Scrambled Eggs

"**N**ature has loud opinions," said the motorcycle driver. He was a wiry young man sporting a yellow kerchief around his neck and purple Converse All Stars on his feet. He took a sip of scalding coffee and shook his head. He was surprisingly calm.

"Guess we better take a look," said Olympia Clumpett. "A flame-broiled motorcycle! Could be a hazard, leaking gasoline and all. I'll call Mayor Grass at the town clerk's office. He might want to put out a call for the volunteer fire departments over at Sharon or Strafford to stand by on the alert, since one of our fire engines has had to take early retirement."

Bucky Clumpett finished heaving a side of beef into the walk-in refrigerator. "Most folks park in front," said Bucky. "What made you scoot around in back? If you were hiding from lightning, you weren't very lucky."

"It's fate," murmured the driver. "Maybe it's all for the best."

"I'll say," said Bucky. "We got gas tanks underground in the front. Lightning strikes *that*, Hamlet is history. Tell you what. We'll refund you the cost of the coffee."

"What's your name, young man?" asked Olympia Clumpett. "Where were you going?"

"None of your business. I don't have to tell you a thing." The motorcyclist began to look nervous. "You don't need to know."

"I mean, are you going to want a ride somewhere?" she explained. "The Greyhound bus only stops here twice a year: once in September to take kids to college and once in late May to bring them home. This is March. You'll have an awfully long wait if you want to use public transportation."

"I'll hitch a ride. Don't worry about me."

"Don't you want me to call the Orange County sheriff?" asked Bucky Clumpett. "If you're going to file an insurance claim—"

"Don't bother," said the driver. But before he could explain why not, another customer barreled into the store. It was a kid, a big kid with blond curls. "Did I just hear some explosion?" he said. "Wow, that was chili powder meets the Death Star, bigtime. What blew up back there?"

"A motorcycle," said Olympia Clumpett.

"I guess I better take a look," said the motorcyclist reluctantly. "Get it over with."

"Come on back," said Bucky, crooking a finger. The fellow walked past the counter and on through the storeroom. The big kid and Olympia joined them. They all stood and stared out the door, while the heavens opened and the backyard of Clumpett's store streamed with rain.

"Peeeeeee-yoooo-ey!" said the boy. "Smells like toilet backup out here."

The Clumpetts couldn't contradict him. The wreckage smelled rotten, and it looked worse. The motorcycle was little more than twisted metal. On the carrier rack smoldered the remains of a steel-reinforced briefcase. It was runny with slimy egg liquids, flecked with fragments of brownish eggshell. The downpour made the amniotic fluid bubble and run off, revealing sad little outlines of bone structure. "You're making an egg delivery in a *briefcase?*" said Bucky Clumpett. "Musta been some millionaire chicken laid those babies."

"Each and every one destroyed?" Ignoring the rain, the motorcyclist squatted down to see. "I think so. It's hard to tell." He touched the broken domes, to see if he could fit them together. "There were seven. Do you think there are seven scrambled eggs here?"

"I make it a rule never to try to unscramble a scrambled egg," said Olympia. "It can't be done, and life is too short."

"Life was too short for *them,*" said Bucky. "Poor little chicks."

"Maybe we're all better off, though," said the motorcyclist, almost under his breath.

Mr. Bucky Clumpett went to the refrigerated case and returned with a carton of Vermont's Finest Fresh Eggs, Extra Large. They were smooth and cool and perfect. "I got in an extra load of white eggs this week, because it's the annual egg decorating and egg hunt in Ethan Allen Park. You can have these. On the house."

"Thanks. But I don't need them."

"They're grand eggs," said Bucky Clumpett stoutly.

"Reared from good-natured Vermont hens who mind their own business."

Olympia said, "While you guys discuss the virtues of Vermont hens, I'm going to dial up our insurance agent, in case there's other damage to the property we haven't noticed yet. We may have to get the constable over here to have a look-see."

At the mention of the constable, the motorcyclist began to back away. The kid said, "I want one of those half-formed skeletons." He splashed through the puddles toward the wreck, his fingers twitching. But before he could get there, another voice came at them from inside the store.

"Thaddeus Nero Tweed!" said the voice.

They all turned. In a modest gray coat with a silk rose pinned to the lapel, a woman was approaching. Despite the gloomy weather, she wore sunglasses with lenses darker than Olympia's home-brewed coffee. Her shoes were sensible. With impatience, she rapped the point of an umbrella against the open back door. "I asked you to come in here and find out which way to the grade school. I did not care to have to follow you in. You know this." Her voice was splendidly posh, almost musical. The accent seemed slightly English. "I beg your pardon. We're looking for"—she consulted a slip of paper—"the Josiah Fawcett Elementary School."

"You sure you don't want the high school?" said Bucky, sizing up the boy.

"I asked about the location of the grade school."

"Well, you're nearly there," said Bucky. "You can almost see it from here. It's just up the road a piece, direction of Crank's Corners. You can't miss it."

"Hey, lady," said the motorcyclist, "if you're heading out of town, could I hitch a ride? My motorcycle's history."

She looked down her narrow nose at him, a glance that took its time to land. "Oh, that's *so* out of the question," she concluded. Then she lifted her umbrella and pointed it at her son. "Return to the car, Thaddeus," she said. "Good morning, all." She swept out of the store.

The boy followed, his face reddening. As the others watched him leave, they saw a state cruiser wheel into the center of Hamlet. It circled the green and came to a stop in front of Clumpett's General Store. "News travels fast," said Bucky Clumpett. "Hey, where are you going?"

The motorcyclist was splashing through the rain that, as the Clumpetts watched, was turning back into a late winter snow. By the time the officer came in, the motorcyclist had disappeared.

"Name is Trooper Crawdad," said the newcomer. "Like to ask you a few questions if I might. You probably see everybody who comes to town."

"Everybody who comes and everybody who goes," said Bucky Clumpett. "Let me get you a cup of coffee, friend, and you can ask away."

Olympia Clumpett went outside. Slowly the mess on the motorcycle was being buried under a blanket of snow. She could still make out the faint line of a backbone, the tender articulations of developing vertebrae. "Good night, sweet chicks," said Olympia Clumpett sadly.

3. Thud Tweed

Miss Earth said, "Never mind the snow, children. It'll change to rain in a minute and run off. Don't worry. We can have our relay race tomorrow. Meanwhile, let's talk about the Spring Egg Hunt."

"Miss Earth," said Sammy Grubb, "isn't an Easter egg hunt a bit silly for people our age?"

"Maybe so and maybe no," said Miss Earth. "This year the egg hunt is a fundraiser to help buy the town a new fire engine. The more people you sign up to sponsor you at twenty-five cents an egg, and the more eggs you find, the more money you can contribute to a good cause."

"First we dye the eggs and hide them, and then we get to find them?" asked Salim Bannerjee. He had moved from India to Vermont last September, and he was still learning the ways of American life. "It seems a total waste of time as well as a lot of fun."

"You children don't hide them," said Miss Earth. "The town selectmen do. They tuck the colored eggs anywhere

11

they like around the common and the buildings in the center of Hamlet. Then, on Saturday morning, all traffic through Hamlet is halted. For an hour the grade-school kids have free range of the whole of Hamlet center."

"Do we buy the eggs we dye?" asked Fawn Petros.

"No," said Miss Earth. "Clumpett's General Store and the Grand Union supermarket donate the eggs. Each class in the school competes to see if its members can find the most eggs."

As she was speaking, the door opened. A biggish boy stood there.

"I'm looking for Earth's class," he said.

"I'm Miss Earth," said Miss Earth, and then her face brightened. "Oh, you must be the new boy. I was expecting you earlier this morning. You're late. But do come in." She turned to the class. "I have a wonderful surprise for you. We have a new student joining us today. His name"—she looked down at a note on her desk—"is Thaddeus Tweed."

"Thaddeus Nero Tweed, if you really want to know," said the boy. "My initials are TNT. But if I bothered to have any friends, I'd make them call me Thud. That would be my nickname."

"You'll have friends here," said Miss Earth. She waved the new boy in. "Don't be bashful. Come right in."

"Why bother? Why don't I move my desk out here in the hall and sit down? I'll get in trouble and you'll just be moving me out here by lunchtime anyway. Let's save time. In fact, I'd like to apply to be expelled right away. What's the worst thing I could do to earn expulsion? Put those goldfish in your tea and make fish soup in the microwave?"

Miss Earth laughed. "What a madcap sense of humor.

Zany and edgy. You'll be right at home. This is your desk. You may sit here in front while we get to know you, Thaddeus."

"Thud," said the boy. "Call me Thud. Thud's the name and Thud's the game." He thudded into the room. He was almost bigger than Miss Earth. He thudded into his desk. The wooden seat screeched in protest.

"Let's get to know one another, shall we?" said Miss Earth. She checked her notes. "You're from Manhattan, I see. By way of introduction, let's all tell each other about ourselves. Would you like to start?"

"No, thank you," said Thud Tweed.

Miss Earth perched on her desk and swung her legs. "What I actually meant was: Introduce yourself to us. It's not an invitation but an assignment."

Thud raked his fingers through his curls and considered. "I ought to be halfway through middle school by now, but I stayed back. That's why I'm bigger than anyone else in this room." He said it evenly, but the message—was it vaguely . . . threatening? "*Much* bigger," he added.

"Where do you live now?" asked Miss Earth.

"My mom just bought a house on Squished Toad Road," said Thud.

"I see," said Miss Earth. "I didn't know there was any property up that way for sale." Then she said, "Unless . . . You don't mean the old Munning house?"

"The place with pillars in front and a tennis court in the backyard? That's it."

"I hear that's a beautiful house," said Miss Earth encouragingly. "I'm sure you'll be happy there."

"I wouldn't bet on it," said Thud. "But it doesn't really

matter. Mom has an incurable illness, and she distracts herself from the constant pain by moving every few months. And Dad doesn't care. He edits an art magazine in Milan. That's a city in Italy," he said to Miss Earth's class. "Italy is a boot kicking Spain in the—"

"That'll do for starters," said Miss Earth quickly. "Now it's our turn to introduce ourselves briefly to Thaddeus. Considering ourselves alphabetically, Salim, you may start."

But before Salim Bannerjee could begin, the intercom pinged. The throat of Principal Buttle was heard clearing itself. "Hello? Miss Earth? I have Mrs. Tweed in the office to see you. Come in, Earth."

"I'm at work," said Miss Earth, enunciating toward the ceiling. "I arrived early today to meet Mrs. Tweed, but she wasn't here yet. Can she come back after school?"

"She says she got lost," said Principal Buttle.

"Her medication makes her a bit fuzzy," remarked Thud, to no one in particular.

The principal added, "She says she can't come back later."

"Her therapy sessions last four hours a day," murmured Thud. "A sad case."

"Well, I'll be right there," said Miss Earth, sighing, "but only briefly."

"Roger. Over and out."

Miss Earth frowned. "Class, I'll have to rely on you to do the introductions in our friendliest Vermont way. Please tell Thaddeus a little about yourselves and make him feel right at home." She aimed a blazing smile at Thud and left the room.

The kids were silent. Somehow Thud made *them* feel shy

instead of the other way around. Maybe because he was so big.

"Well, go on, make some noise in my direction. I'm bored already," said Thud.

Salim stood up next to his desk. "I'm Salim Bannerjee. I was the newest kid in the class until you came along. You'll like it here. I do."

"Your name is Slim? You look slim. You look like a weakling."

"No, not Slim. It's Sa-LEEM. Sa-LEEM."

"What a stupid name. What a funny accent. Where do you come from?"

"The Indian subcontinent."

"No wonder they call it a subcontinent, then," said Thud. "Subnormal, if they breed folks like you."

The children's mouths dropped open. "That's not funny," said Salim.

"So remind me to cut that line out of my opening routine. Next?"

Salim sat down. Nina stood up and said, "I'm Nina Bueno. My family came from Honduras."

"What is this, the United Nations' kiddie division?" said Thud.

Nina explained. "You see, just across the Connecticut River from us, over in New Hampshire, are Dartmouth College and Locust Computer Labs. They employ workers from Hamlet and other places."

"I'd rather be from Hamlet," said Thud. "*Far* from Hamlet."

"Are you trying to be funny or mean? Hamlet is a great place to live," replied Nina. "Ask any cow or dog or person."

"Which one are you?" said Thud.

"Moo," said Nina. "Bow wow. Mind your manners. Guess."

Before things got nasty, Moshe Cohn leaped to his feet in a gentlemanly way. "I'm Moshe Cohn, My dad is a doctor."

"Don't worry, he'll find a cure for you sooner or later," said Thud.

"That's insulting," said Moshe.

"You noticed," said Thud. "Bright boy. You'll go far. You can start right now." He pointed toward the door.

"I'm Carly Garfunkel," said a girl. "Don't say anything nasty to me, or I'll—"

Thud made a rude gesture but kept his mouth shut. He also pinched his nose with his fingers as if Carly had just produced an unpleasant odor.

A boy stood up. He had a baseball cap stuffed in the back pocket of his jeans. He didn't look alarmed. He looked cool. And he looked coolly at Thud and said, "I'm the Chief of the Copycats, a club of boys from this classroom. Grubb's the name. Sammy Grubb."

"Isn't a grub like a maggot?" said Thud. "Doesn't a grub, like, chew on rotting flesh?"

"If you're not sure, look it up and get back to me," said Sammy Grubb. "I am Grubb with two b's. You want to join the Copycats, see me at recess. I'll review your application. Miss Earth doesn't like her students to hang around in clubs. So as Copycats, we boys try to conduct our club's activities outside the classroom, to respect Miss Earth's feelings."

"Respecting a teacher's feelings? Are you all nuts here?"

"I'll save the rest of the history of the Copycats for another time. You know where to find me."

"Yeah, but where can I lose you?" said Thud.

"Hard to do," Sammy shot back, "since I'm not a loser."

A girl with long braids stood up. "I'm Pearl Hotchkiss," she said, "and I don't belong to the Copycats, since I'm not a boy."

"Could've fooled me," said Thud.

"Thanks for the compliment," she replied. "I don't belong to the Tattletales either, which is the girls' club in this room. I'm a free agent and a solo act."

Thud raised his eyebrows. For once he didn't look bored. "Is that so?" he said. "Hey, maybe we should get together and start our own club, skinnylegs."

"I don't do clubs," Pearl said. She looked at her legs as she sat down. They didn't look skinny. They looked just right.

Lois Kennedy the Third said, "Excuse me if I don't stand. I don't think you deserve that much respect. I'm Lois Kennedy the Third."

"Are you related to the presidential Kennedys? If so, when are you planning on dying?"

Stuttering was coming from all over the room. None of the students had ever heard such a mouth on a kid. They didn't know what to say. If they registered their dislike, Thud Tweed might attempt bodily harm. There was an awful lot of him to try it. "Go on," he said to Anna Maria. "I might as well learn the worst. Who are you?"

"Anna Maria Mastrangelo," said Anna Maria in a clipped voice, as if not to give Thud any information he could tease her with.

"Forest Eugene Mopp," said Forest, "the resident Mr. Science."

"Thekla Mustard," said Thekla Mustard.

"Thekla? THECK-la?"

"You got it," said Thekla.

"*Theck* to rhyme with Wreck? *La,* a note to follow *Sol?* THECK-LA?"

"Not Theeeek-la, not Theckles, not Teekla, not Tickles," said Thekla. "Get it right or don't use it at all. I am the legally elected Empress of the Tattletales, a club that you are not invited to join. The Tattletales is a *girls'* club."

"I see," said Thud politely. "I wish it well."

Thekla looked suspicious but sat down.

"Thekla MUSTARD," said Thud amazedly. "The *people* you have here in Vermont!"

"Fawn Petros," said Fawn in a small voice. "Nothing to add."

"Mike Saint Michael," said Mike. "A regular joe."

"Stan Tomaski," said Stan. "Ditto."

"Sharday Wren," said Sharday. "I am the best dancer in the school. Why they call you Thud?"

"'Cause when I dance, that's what it sounds like," he said. He looked around. "Hmm, so here's how it stacks up. Counting skinnylegs there, eight girls. Counting me, seven boys."

"Eight boys—Hector Yellow is absent today," said Sammy Grubb. "So now the number of boys and girls in the class is even. Eight each. Seven boys in the Copycats and one boy not yet admitted to membership. Seven girls in the Tattletales and one girl who won't enroll. A balance of power at last."

Sammy had a gleam in his eye. If Thud Tweed could be encouraged to join the Copycats, they'd finally outnumber the Tattletales. It would be only a numerical superiority, but any superiority was better than none. Also, thought Sammy, it would be better to have the hulking Thud as a club member than as an enemy or rival. Less dangerous. "You should really think about joining the Copycats, Thud," said Sammy. "We could use some new blood."

"I'm good at providing blood," said Thud. "Just watch me."

He smiled at them all quickly. A toothy smile, cold and mysterious. Just as swiftly, it was gone. He went back to looking like a slab of baby bison crammed into a school desk. Like a thundercloud positively packed with lightning.

4. Must a Bad Seed
Become a Bad Weed?

At Clumpett's General Store, Trooper Crawdad finished his coffee and took a few notes about the lightning-struck motorcycle. Then he phoned headquarters. Trooper Crawdad reported the events of the morning.

"To be on the safe side," said Trooper Crawdad, "I suppose an all-points bulletin ought to be posted. Be on the lookout for speeding motorcyclists with briefcases secured on their racks. Just in case this one I found in Hamlet isn't the right one."

"I'll put it out on the waves," said his superior officer.

"Thanks," said Trooper Crawdad. "Einfinger said that losing the contents of his briefcase might pose a threat to national security. Should we alert the feds?"

"If it's a real threat, Einfinger will be in touch with the FBI himself."

"Guess so. Over and out."

Olympia Clumpett said to her husband, "I've checked

high and low. Can't smell any smoldering timbers in the attic or see any scorched paint around the electrical outlets. Looks like we were spared, though the poor bike and its luggage didn't do so well."

Trooper Crawdad interrupted. "I'm still puzzling over the case."

"Which case? The briefcase?"

He laughed. "In this case, I mean both the briefcase and the case of the stolen briefcase. I tend to doubt this is the same bike that stole the briefcase out of Professor Einfinger's trunk. Eggs aren't vital to our national security, far as I know. And who would steal eggs?"

"Still, that motorcycle fellow sure lit outta here fast when you showed up," said Bucky Clumpett. "So go figure."

"Well, I'll have Lorraine at headquarters run Einfinger's license plate through the computer and get a phone number and give the fellow a call. Let him know what we got here." Trooper Crawdad thanked the Clumpetts for the coffee. They wouldn't accept payment, so he put four quarters in the glass jar that was collecting spare change for the new fire engine.

Miss Earth approached the woman who stood in the lobby of the Josiah Fawcett Elementary School. "You must be Thaddeus's mother. I'm his teacher. My name is Germaine Earth."

"Oh," said the woman. "Yes, I'm Mrs. Tweed."

"Please, Hamlet is such a small town—you might as well call me Germaine," said Miss Earth.

Mrs. Tweed looked reluctant to give out her own first name, but then she sighed. "Well, I suppose you can call me

Mildred." Though the clouds were still low and the light was poor, she didn't remove her dark glasses. Maybe her poorly condition made her eyes sensitive to overhead lights.

"I can take only a few moments away from my class," said Miss Earth. "But perhaps we can schedule a chatter for some time after school."

"I'm a very private woman," said Mrs. Tweed. "I don't chatter. But look here. I want to apologize in advance for anything my son does. You have my permission to keep him after school." She opened her leather purse with a click. "I'd like to give you a blank check to pay for any damage."

"Damage?" said Miss Earth. "What sort of damage?"

"Oh, computers frying, windows breaking. Any therapy you might have to seek for yourself. Or maybe you'll want to give him special tutoring. Charge what you like; it's worth it." Mrs. Tweed scrawled an illegible signature on a check.

"Mrs. Tweed . . . Mildred. Perhaps I ought to make the time to go into the teachers' lounge. Perhaps you'd like to sit down." She looked at Mrs. Tweed sympathetically. "We won't chatter. We'll confer. It sounds as if I ought to know a little bit more about your son."

"Miss Earth, you haven't listened. All I want to say, I can say right now."

Mrs. Tweed elaborated her syllables with the perky tones of privilege. "I've tried *every* kind of schooling for Thaddeus except for prison, and I'd try that if he were old enough to qualify. He's been in public schools and private schools. He's been in military academies in Virginia and in boarding schools in Switzerland. The Jesuits threw him out. The Franciscans threw him out. The good Sisters of Mercy brought charges against him. I'm at my wits' end. Finally I thought: Maybe we'll try a dull rural setting."

Hamlet is anything but dull, thought Miss Earth, thinking about the events of the school year so far: infestations of poisonous spiders, manifestations of mammoth ghosts, visitations by aliens from space, to say nothing of the general romance in the air. But she shook her head and went back to listening to Mrs. Tweed.

"Can you understand this, Miss Earth? Can you manage him for a month or two? I'm sure when it gets too much, we can move again, but if we could just stick it out here until the end of the school year—under cover, as it were—I'd be grateful."

She didn't want to admit to her devastating illness. How brave of her. "Mildred Tweed," said Miss Earth, "he seems a nice enough boy. What exactly is it about your child?"

"Don't ask me. I haven't time to go into it more deeply." She looked at the snow as it turned back to rain. She undid her scarf to retie it more tightly about her head. For a woman with a society voice and manner, her hair was cut surprisingly close, almost a buzzcut. It had the flat color of a manila envelope.

"If you're all that busy, maybe I should speak with Thaddeus's father," said Miss Earth. "I'll need his phone number. Thaddeus said he spends most of the year in Milan."

"Oh, did he?" said Mrs. Tweed. "And you believed him?"

"Oh, I see," said Miss Earth, a little sadly.

After a pause, Mrs. Tweed looked at her hands and said, "Mr. Tweed is deceased. Permanently."

"Oh, dear. Poor Thaddeus. Poor boy."

"Yes," said Mrs. Tweed. "No doubt his father's absence is the cause of Thaddeus's bad behavior. But there you are."

"And things are all right with you?" said Miss Earth, proud of how she worded that, so it could seem a delicate inquiry into Mrs. Tweed's health if she chose to hear it that way. But she did not so choose.

"Do your best with Thaddeus," said Mrs. Tweed concludingly. "He's a big boy with big clumsy ways. Don't let on that you're scared, and stay out of his way. That's my advice to you. And if you can hold him here more than a month, you'll be setting a modern record."

"Your son has had a few sad times. Some hard knocks. But he can change. That's what life is all about, Mildred. Education, too. It's about change."

"Change for the worse, sometimes," said Mrs. Tweed. "Sometimes I fear he's just a bad seed." She paused and lowered her dark glasses. For an instant Miss Earth caught sight of iridescent green eyes, beautiful but troubled. "And bad seeds grow up to be—well, bad weeds."

"Not on my watch," said Miss Earth staunchly, throwing back her shoulders. "A bad seed? Not in my vocabulary."

"Oh, well. You'll learn," said Mrs. Tweed. "I retain the best legal counsel, Miss Earth, in case my son's behavior returns him to the juvenile courts."

"Mildred," said Miss Earth, "before you go, just tell me this. Thaddeus introduced himself as Thud. Do you approve of our calling him that nickname, or would you rather we avoid it? What do you call him?"

Mrs. Tweed had already turned and walked out of the school. A chauffeur opened the door of her town car, which

24

had been parked in the bus lane despite signs forbidding anyone from stopping there. Mrs. Tweed called over her shoulder, "I call him Thud, yes. I do."

Oh, my, thought Miss Earth. Just what I need to enliven my dull and listless days in the dull little hamlet of Hamlet. A challenge.

But, good teacher that she was, she was determined to meet this challenge.

5. Join the Club!

When Miss Earth came back into her classroom, she looked her usual self, calm and competent. "Introductions are all done, I trust?" she said. "Well, let's get back to our earlier topic. The annual Spring Egg Hunt this weekend is for a good cause. The town of Hamlet sorely needs a new fire engine. So may I have a show of hands to indicate how many of you intend to take part in this fundraiser?"

Everyone in the class raised a hand except for Stan Tomaski, Pearl Hotchkiss, and Thud Tweed.

"It's my weekend to go visit my father in Cohoes," said Stan. "I won't be back in time."

"I have to babysit," said Pearl. "I always have to babysit. So many younger kids in my family."

"And Thud?" said Miss Earth.

"I'm not interested," said Thud.

"It would be a chance to get to know your classmates," she said brightly.

"Sadly, I think I have to be in Central America this

weekend," he replied. "My mom does this monthly transfusion thing in some fleabag hospital in a third-world country because the process is illegal in the U.S."

"We'll miss you. Perhaps you can do a special report on your trip. Well, class, we've used up all the time we have now. The recess bell will ring in a minute. After recess, we'll head for the cafeteria and hard-boil those eggs and dye them for Sunday. Yes, Thekla?"

Thekla Mustard stood up. "Miss Earth," she said, "I propose that the girls and the boys in this classroom have our own private contest to see which group can find the most eggs."

"Oh, I don't—"

"I know you don't like competitions, but this egg hunt is *already* competitive, class by class. Pitting *our* classroom against itself, boys versus the girls, will encourage us to make our best efforts," said Thekla. "You can't doubt it. And it *is* for the fire engine. A noble cause and all that."

Sammy Grubb popped to his feet and said, "Miss Earth, it isn't fair. Thekla's only proposing this because she just heard that Stan isn't going to be here and Thud doesn't want to do it. So we boys are outnumbered. There'll be only six of us, and there'll be seven girls. Of course, we'd win anyway, since boys rule and girls drool."

"Girls don't drool," said Thekla primly. "We *chomp*."

"Children," said Miss Earth, "I don't think so—"

Thud tilted his desk back on two legs, and with his big boots he ground the edges of Pearl's pigtails into the back of her seat.

"Cut it out," said Pearl.

"Why not allow the boys-girls competition? What's

wrong with a little fun?" Thud said. "Maybe if it sounded like more fun, I might agree to show up."

Miss Earth frowned. "And leave your mother to endure her transfusion in Central America alone? Surely not."

"She'd probably prefer it that way. I get on her nerves in a big way."

Miss Earth was stuck. She didn't approve of the endless rivalry between girls and boys in her class. On the other hand, this new student had made a suggestion and seemed interested. It was her job to make him feel at home. "Well," she said at last, "whatever you decide. I just don't want to know about it. I only want to hear the *total* amount my classroom earns for the fire engine fund." The bell rang. "The threat of lightning has passed, so we can have outdoor recess. Line up, class."

The rain kept changing into snowflakes and the snowflakes back into rain again. Miss Earth's class ran to one side of the yard, where Mayor Grass had plowed the snow into a private range of Himalayas to play on. Today the slopes of winter were turning into the swamps of spring.

The kids were nervous to see what the new boy would do.

Thud Tweed idled. He sidled. He sallied. He dallied. He loitered near the kindergartners and loomed so large over them that they got scared and went to huddle near their teacher, Ms. Frazzle. She looked up from the vacation brochures she was reading with interest. She scowled at Thud. "Do you have a visitor's pass?" she said to him.

"I'm not a visitor, I'm an inmate," said Thud. "I go here now."

Ms. Frazzle realized her mistake. "Oh. You're large for your age," she said.

"Well, you're old for your size," he answered. As Ms. Frazzle was trying to work out whether or not this was an insult, Thud sauntered away.

Lois Kennedy the Third was watching with a keener eye than the others. With the coming of spring, she felt a renewal of her lifelong ambition to unseat Thekla Mustard as Empress of the Tattletales. Thekla had been Empress for the entire life of the club, which had started when they were kids in Ms. Frazzle's kindergarten class. It was no fair. Was there a way to turn the arrival of Thud Tweed into a crisis of Tattletale leadership? Maybe Lois could irritate Thekla into calling for a vote of confidence. Maybe this time Lois would win the Empress-ship at last. It was worth a try.

The Tattletales were busy chewing over their favorite subject: Was their teacher engaged to Mayor Tim Grass or not? She was wearing a ring these days. Lois interrupted the discussion and called a huddle. All the Tattletales flocked together and stitched their arms through one another's, making a circle to keep their remarks private.

"I have an idea," said Lois. "Let's try to recruit that Thud boy as a Tattletale."

The girls all laughed until Thekla said briskly, "*Quiet.*" She glanced around. "Lois, let me point out the obvious. The Tattletales is an exclusive girls' club, made up of exclusive girls. We exclude boys. Thud is a boy. Therefore it follows that Thud can't be a Tattletale. Am I going too fast for you?"

"We've always been a girls' club," said Lois, "but maybe Miss Earth is right. Isn't that boy-girl competition a bit stale? We're getting older. We're changing. We can deal. Besides, if we could recruit Thud, we'd finally outnumber the Copycats entirely."

"But he's a behemoth," said Thekla. "Look at him. He's a mound of juvenile delinquency. He's dangerous. He's powerful."

"We could use someone powerful in the Tattletales," said Lois.

"We have *me*," said Thekla with steely clarity.

"Oh, you. How powerful are you?" asked Lois, looking her in the eye.

"Powerful enough," said Thekla. "Don't push me, Lois." She looked Lois right back in the eye. Since Thekla wore glasses, the effect was more intense. Lois backed down once again. She unstitched her arms and walked away as if uninterested in the Tattletales anymore. What she was interested in, of course, was legitimate power. She went and stood behind the Dumpster, trying to come up with a plan.

On the other side of the huge snowbank the Copycats were having an informal chat.

"Should we persuade Thud to join the Copycats?" asked Salim Bannerjee.

"I've been rethinking my offer. Could we handle it?" said Sammy Grubb. "He does seem like a troublemaker."

"Perhaps he's just lonely," said Salim. "And scared. I felt scared last September when I came to this school for the first time. You all knew each other so well. You'd all lived in fascinating Hamlet, Vermont, your whole lives, while I had lived only in boring old Bombay, India. I was happy when you invited me to join the Copycats. I felt less alone. Maybe he would, too."

"We don't want to invite a junior terrorist," said Mike.

"We could just ask him on a trial basis, at least for the egg hunt," said Salim. "Poor guy."

"He's not poor," said Moshe. "He lives at the old Munning estate. That's huge. His folks must be loaded."

"Even rich people can be lonely," said Salim. "So I hear. You were nice to me. You should be nice to him, too."

The boys watched Thud rush into a puddle and stamp all its water into the air, making a group of second-grade girls shriek and cover their faces. "I'm not sure it's a good idea, if none of us even has the nerve to go ask him," said Forest Eugene.

Salim said, "Sammy, you had the courage to invite *me* to join the Copycats when I moved here. I should follow your good example." He straightened his shoulders and went over to talk to Thud.

They stood too far away for the other Copycats to hear. Lois, however, was still scheming behind the Dumpster. She listened carefully.

"Why should I join a club called the Copycats?" Thud was saying. "I hate boys almost more than I hate girls."

"Well, you might hate most boys, but these boys are likable," said Salim. "I was scared of them when I arrived from Bombay in September, but they were nice to me. So I like them."

"They were nice to you?" said Thud. "Hah. They probably made fun of that fake English accent you have."

"I don't have any fake accent," said Salim. "It's my real accent."

"They probably think you're a weirdo," said Thud. "I would if I hadn't met any other Indians before. My dad runs a gambling casino in Calcutta, though, and I know his minions pretty well. Don't you realize why these hayseeds were nice to you?"

"Good manners," said Salim.

"Nope. They roped you into the ranks of the Copycats just because they wanted to have the same number of members as the Tattletales. They'd have taken any dork from Dindia or any jerk from Jindia or any schmuck from Schmindia. They didn't care who you were. They only cared that you were a boy and could help them balance the voting strength of the Copycats with the Tattletales."

"How do you know this?" said Salim.

"Common sense. Now the Copycats want to outnumber the Tattletales at last. I've been expecting someone to come over and egg me into joining. Hardly thought it would be you, though. You're even more of a pushover than you look."

"I'm not a pushover," said Salim.

"You think they like you, don't you?" said Thud. "If I marched over there and said I'd join the club if you were kicked out, I bet they'd go for it."

"They never would!" said Salim. "They've been my friends through thick and thin."

"You dare me to?" said Thud.

Salim didn't dare. Shaking his head, he just walked away from Thud.

But Lois, peering around the side of the Dumpster, thought Salim looked uneasy.

6. The Bad Egg

After recess, Miss Earth said, "Now, class, soon we'll be heading down to the cafeteria to help our kindergarten pals dye their eggs. Ms. Frazzle will supervise. I have to go to the office to pick up your sponsor forms, so I want you all to be on your best behavior."

Salim Bannerjee raised his hand. "Miss Earth," he asked, "when I lived in Bombay, I saw eggs in the shop windows every spring. They were painted with bland colors and cradled in nests of grass. But since my father is a Bangladeshi Hindu and my mother is a Muslim, I never learned why western people bother to paint eggs."

"Who would like to tell Salim a little bit about American spring celebrations and the lore of Easter eggs?" said Miss Earth.

No one would. No one knew anything about it.

"Spring is a happy season for all living things," said Miss Earth. "Human communities rely on the growing seasons in spring and summer to feed themselves and their livestock, so that they may have corn and wheat from the fields, vegetables from the garden, fruit from the orchards and waysides, and dairy products and meat from their cattle. Think what a joy it is to shuck off your overcoat on a sunny afternoon, and to see the grass greening out of its brown death. The buds blurt open. The birds return. The bees buzz at their jobs. The world gets interested in itself again." Miss Earth was getting rhapsodic.

"But why *eggs* as a symbol?" asked Pearl Hotchkiss.

"Hens lay eggs. Those that are fertilized hatch into chicks," said Miss Earth. "I imagine our ancestors saw eggs sitting around in the sun and considered them to be as lifeless as stones. Then, one day, presto! The stone appears to crack. The shell of the egg is destroyed from the inside out. Here comes a little beak, here peers an eye, here emerges a new creature, stepping out, drying in the sun. Life appears to emerge from nonlife. If it weren't so real, it would be magic. We celebrate the egginess of the spring holidays, including Easter, because we are, deep down, relieved that the world, as if by magic, has come back to life again."

"It's not Easter yet, though," said Anna Maria Mastrangelo. "Not for several weeks."

"This is called a Spring Egg Hunt, so as not to interfere with Easter plans, and also to include everyone," said Miss Earth. "Spring belongs to *all*." With one hand, she steadied herself on her desk. She was partial to this season. "Perhaps we should take a moment to write down what we love best about the springtime," she said.

"What I love best about the springtime is the annual broadcast of the Academy Awards," said Thud. "I love to watch hopeful people lose. And in front of an audience of billions, too. It's very rewarding."

The class laughed, but uneasily.

This brought Miss Earth back to earth. "Line up, class," she said, a bit tartly.

"I still don't know why we paint eggs," said Salim. But Miss Earth was in no mood to pursue this line of enquiry at the moment. "While I'm in the office, I want you to behave in the cafeteria," she said. "I mean it."

The cafeteria was a scene of mayhem. Mrs. Brill, the lunch lady, teetered on a stool in the school kitchen, lowering a wire basket full of white eggs into a vat of boiling water. Around her, the kindergarten kids were shrieking in anticipation. "Sit down, I tell you, or you'll be scalded with splashing water and disfigured for life!" screamed Mrs. Brill. She adored holidays except for the dangers involved in observing them.

Ms. Frazzle, the kindergarten teacher, said, "Now, children, come over here. While we're waiting, I'll read you a story. *Little Bunny Dyes Her Eggs.*"

"Oh, shoot," said Thud in a loud voice. "Why don't you read the sequel, the one simply called *Little Bunny Dies?*"

The kindergartners liked the Little Bunny books. They began to weep at the thought that Little Bunny could die.

"Well, it's seasonal," said Thud. "I mean, if coloring eggs is to celebrate life, you have to balance it with the notion of death. Don't you?"

"Are you a bad egg?" said Ms. Frazzle. "Look here, big kid, don't think because I teach kindergarten that I don't have any muscle. I was the stunt double for Linda Hamilton in *Terminator 2.*" She wasn't really, but she didn't like the look of Thud.

Mrs. Brill brayed, "Eggs are done! Let me just cool them down!" She placed the basket in a vat of cold water. "I have gotten out the dyes and the vinegar and the spoons and the paper towels. Every kindergartner gets to do three eggs."

"Join your pals, pals," said Ms. Frazzle. Miss Earth's kids scattered to find their junior partners.

"I don't have a pal," said Thud. "But it's okay—I don't want one."

"You can hand out the eggs," said Ms. Frazzle. "Carefully, please."

"Absolutely," said Thud. He took the basket from Mrs. Brill and began to hop like a huge, insane monster rabbit. Four eggs fell out and smashed on the floor. "Oops," said Thud. "Dead eggs."

The kindergartners began to cry again.

"You: Be careful," said Ms. Frazzle, "or I'll break something of *yours.*"

The children settled to their work. The kindergartners began to be happy again. They dipped their eggs in yellow and purple, in red and blue, in orange and green. When they were done, Ms. Frazzle led them back to the kindergarten, singing bunny carols.

Mrs. Brill returned with another basket of hard-boiled eggs. "Now it's your turn," she said to Miss Earth's students. "I've brought out the good paints and brushes. Settle down and do some nice work. You're a lively bunch; come through with something original."

"I'm not lively," said Thud. "I'm deadly."

"Spring is the time of change," said Mrs. Brill. "So

change." In her right hand she held an enormous industrial metal ladle. It looked heavy as a crowbar. Thud chose not to reply.

"Do we paint anything special?" asked Salim.

"When I was small," Mrs. Brill told them, "my family had a custom at egg-dyeing time. We children painted and drew pictures of what we wanted to change into when we grew up. Then we buried the eggs in the garden in the hopes that our wishes would come true."

"Did any of your wishes come true?" asked Fawn Petros in a little voice.

"They did," said Mrs. Brill. "I wanted to be a lunch lady. I married Bob Brill and moved to Hamlet, and the rest is history. So paint your best possible futures, kids. Go for it."

Anna Maria Mastrangelo painted herself as a singing nun.

Forest Eugene Mopp painted himself as a scientist mixing potions.

Thekla Mustard painted herself as the first female dictator of the world.

Pearl Hotchkiss painted herself balancing on a split-rail fence with a straw jauntily poking out between her teeth. Unfortunately, the line wobbled as she drew it, and she looked more like a European countess with a cigarette in a long elegant holder. She hoped she wasn't going to turn into a snob by accident just because of some silly painted egg.

Fawn Petros painted herself as a penguin.

Moshe Cohn painted himself as a heart surgeon.

Nina Bueno painted herself as a hostess on a game show.

Carly Garfunkel painted herself as herself, only bigger in a few important places.

Sammy Grubb dawdled and couldn't decide. Finally he

painted himself with a magnifying glass. If only he could discover Bigfoot or the Loch Ness Monster or some dinosaurs that escaped from a Steven Spielberg movie. It was his life's goal.

Mike Saint Michael painted himself with a wife and kids. The wife was hiding behind a bunch of flowers, because he didn't want anyone to know who it was. He didn't know who it was, either.

Stan Tomaski painted himself as a star quarterback.

Sharday Wren painted herself as a star ballerina.

Lois Kennedy the Third painted herself as the newly elected Empress of the Tattletales. She had the tall collar of her trench coat pulled up high, and dark glasses settled low on her nose. She looked mean. She didn't care. She *felt* mean. She wanted to *be* mean, if she could manage it. That stupid Thekla Mustard! Why couldn't she take a holiday from world domination once in a while?

Salim Bannerjee painted himself as an Indian prince riding on the howdah of a pet elephant. The elephant came out sort of squished, and it looked more like a pet alligator. Oh, well.

When Miss Earth returned with the egg-hunt sponsor forms, she admired many of the paintings. "What did you do with your egg, Thaddeus? What is your hope for the future?"

The new boy made a fist and brought it down on the egg, mashing its shell. If there was a secret hope painted on it, nobody could see it now. "Thud," he said. "Thud thud thud."

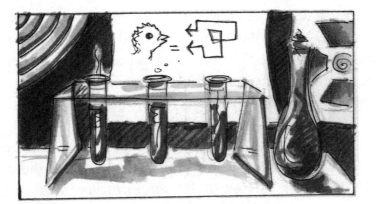

7. Elderthumb and Einfinger

In a high-tech laboratory fortress overlooking Route 128 near Boston, Professor Wolfgang Einfinger's boss was discussing the theft with him.

"Einfinger, this experiment has been six years in development," said Dr. Elderthumb.

"Yes, Doctor," said Einfinger. "But it was only a few eggs—"

"They were important little eggs. Did you not know this?"

"Of course I did," said Einfinger. "At least I understand some of it."

"We were going one step further than little chicks, Einfinger. With a little judicious gene therapy, we were on the edge of what I call 'reverse evolution.' The natural consequence of Elderthumb's Throwback Theory."

"Throwback Theory?" said Einfinger nervously. Elderthumb had never spelled it out before.

"*Elderthumb's* Throwback Theory. The possibility that a

species could be encouraged to revert to an ancestral form. Einfinger, I knew that could I but find the DNA switch, I could coax a cloned embryo of an elephant to remember its family roots as a mastodon! A baby sparrow to grow up and screech in rage like a pterodactyl!"

"*Elderthumb's* Throwback Theory . . . I see."

"But theory and practice are not the same, Einfinger. Imagining something and getting it to work are different jobs. For years I slaved over a hot incubator. Worked my wicked fingers to the bone! Stitching onto your basic chicken double helixes the little bits of DNA clipped from the nucleic blueprints of other critters. I could dress up the raw material just fine, but I couldn't cook 'em to life. I learned that you can't make an omelet without breaking eggs—and buster, did I break 'em!"

"Every night and every day, I suspect. But why wouldn't it work?"

"I couldn't tell. Then, almost as if a wonderful little fairy took pity on poor, tired Elderthumb, we had a breakthrough. An accidental breakthrough. I was fiddling with some old random crusts of DNA from a rare blue-toed lizard, pinching this bit and poking that, when a fire alarm required I leave the lab. *Someone* was smoking in the restroom."

"I've given up cigarettes, Dr. Elderthumb. Much better for my health."

"Whatever. The important thing is that the building was evacuated; the lab was left unsupervised for an hour. Something happened. Maybe some foreign matter tracked in by the fire brigade? Or some careless fireman gave the incubator knobs a twiddle, turning the heat up or down at a significant moment? I can't say. But when we came back, the revised embryos were percolating in their eggshells. Seven little eggs!"

"And we're still in the dark about *why* it began to work."

"We *need* those eggs, Einfinger. We need to watch them hatch. To see what happens. To kill the chicks and dissect them. Autopsies. Examine their bone structures. Their musculature. Look into their innards. Right down into their very cells. Crack the DNA playbook. Hypothesize what we did right. Do it again, only more right."

"But Dr. Elderthumb," said Einfinger, "you said that losing the eggs was a threat to national security. How can that be? Eggs are eggs. A dime a dozen."

"Don't be a noodlehead!" shouted Dr. Elderthumb. "Just listen to me! We are working in a very dicey area here. We're not doing just your run-of-the-mill *cloning*. Cloned creatures are prone to illness. Also premature aging. They're not viable yet as a product. So we're trying something different. We're trying to get back to an ancestor of our modern contemporary up-to-the-minute chicken. And if we can master this, Einfinger—if we can figure out how to engineer reverse-evolution chickens from modern genetically altered chicks—"

"Yes, Dr. Elderthumb."

"Then we work on reverse kangaroos."

"Yes, Dr. Elderthumb."

"What next, Einfinger? Reverse possums? Pussycats? Piglings?"

Professor Einfinger said, "Reverse porcupines, maybe?"

Dr. Elderthumb slowly stood up. "No. *People*, Einfinger. Reverse *humans*. Think of it. A revolution in the work force.

Move the human being back to where it has an opposable thumb but no opposable brain. Think of the possibilities! Can you think of them?"

Wolfgang Einfinger was too nervous to answer.

"I'm talking moola-moola, Einfinger! Filthy lucre. Big bucks. Mega smackeroos. What wouldn't the marketplace pay for a work force to do grunt work? These will be human drones. Worker bees. Little more than human ants. Ants in pants. We'll rent them out by the dozens, in cargo containers."

"But the threat to national security?"

"You're a doofusburger! Can't you see? If we can keep our technique secret until we manage to produce a throw-back human, we can present the notion to the government as an endless source of human labor. For the Army. For the Navy. For the Air Force. For a price."

"Tell it to the Marines," murmured Einfinger.

"*Exactly.*"

"But will the U.S. government like the notion of an armed force populated with reversely engineered throwback humans?"

"If they don't, Einfinger, who cares? Surely you've heard of world domination?"

"Oh. Dr. Elderthumb! You're not hoping to be a mad scientist!"

"No, no, no." Dr. Elderthumb blushed. "Not mad. A bit madcap, maybe, but not mad. Simply a good scientist trying to prove a theory. But Einfinger, let me tell you this. I'm mad enough at you to fire you outright and smear your reputation. You'll never work in this field again."

"I'm sorry, Dr. Elderthumb. I stopped to use a men's room. I had a need. We all have needs."

"Indeed we do, Einfinger. And I have a need right now. Find out what happened to those eggs. Track down the motorcycling thief. If those eggs have been destroyed, I want a scrap of the genetic material. A bit of the shell. A scoop of the liquid. I want to see the skeleton of the corpse. Anything. They were far enough along. They won't have deteriorated yet. I don't care if you have to wade up to your ears in a pit of garbage. Find me the remains of those embryonic chicks."

"Yes, Dr. Elderthumb. I'll be in touch with the Vermont State Police—"

"Einfinger! Are you loony tunes? *Don't* get the police involved! If the authorities find out what we're doing, we'll be closed down and spending our summers sunning ourselves in Sing Sing! Keep this out of the papers and off the police records! And that Trooper Crawdad—if you think he's looking for that motorcycle, put him off the job! Throw him off the scent! Or I'll scramble your head in a frying pan!"

Dr. Elderthumb grasped her blackthorn cane and left the room.

Professor Wolfgang Einfinger went back to his office. On his desk was a Post-it note from his secretary. "Call Trooper Hiram Crawdad of the Vermont State Police." Einfinger tried the number, but Trooper Crawdad had already clocked out for the day.

8. The Hunt

When he dialed the Vermont State Police headquarters again the next morning, Einfinger learned that Trooper Crawdad hadn't left the building yet. "I'll put you through," said the receptionist, and in a minute Trooper Crawdad came on the line.

"A *very* good morning to you, officer," said Einfinger in a phony sort of way. "Beautiful day up there in your beautiful state?"

"Overcast. Cold. An icy drizzle. Mud season on its way. Black fly season after that. Yep, pretty beautiful. God's country. How can I help you, sir?"

"Oh, we met yesterday when you stopped me for speeding on I–89. Just near the I–91 interchange, remember? Well, I had been grousing on about a stolen briefcase and a motorcycling thief. But guess what—I went back to the McDonald's in West Lebanon and discovered I'd left the briefcase in the men's room! So it was never stolen after all. So don't worry about it. Just spend your time catching crooks and eating doughnuts and, oh, whatever it is you do so well."

"Gee, Professor," said Trooper Crawdad. "I set out to check town centers within a thirty-mile radius of our little meeting, and I came across an abandoned motorcycle that had been struck by lightning. At first I thought I might have located the vehicle of your thief. But I changed my mind. This bike had a briefcase on the back, but the thing was only filled with broken eggs. I'm sure that for the President a good breakfast is vital to our national security, but otherwise I decided it was a false lead. Thanks for corroborating my conclusion. So long now."

Professor Einfinger was both horrified and delighted. Horrified to learn that the eggs had been destroyed. Delighted to learn that the motorcycle had been located. If that dolt Trooper Crawdad could find it, so could he. And how many town centers could there be within a thirty-mile radius of exit 1 on I–89? A motorcycle struck by lightning was news. Someone would have heard of it. It was only a matter of time before he found it.

He tanked up and bought a map and headed for the Green Mountain State.

That same Thursday morning, Miss Earth's class was outside decorating their egg tree when Mayor Tim Grass drove by the school. He stopped to chew the fat with Miss Earth. All the children watched with interest. Thekla said, "Their lips are less than twelve inches apart. Technically, they must be in love. But are they engaged? That's the question."

"If you're going to talk romance, we're outta here," said Sammy Grubb, and the Copycats took advantage of some downtime to stamp in the warm spring mud and make revolting squelching noises, rather like the sounds of kissing.

Thekla Mustard noticed that Thud wasn't interested in mud noise. He was hanging around the egg tree. He winked at her. She decided he was studying her to see how power was handled by a master. If the right occasion came along, she'd demonstrate it to him. A moment later, it did.

"Thekla," said Lois Kennedy the Third, "I want to nominate myself to be captain of the girls' egg-hunting team."

"Lois," said Thekla, "when will you learn? I'm the powerhouse in the group. I'm in charge. End of story."

"I don't see you wielding much power. Maybe we should have another election."

Thekla took a deep breath. "I've had it with you, Lois. Always trying to unseat me from my throne."

"I just want a chance to rule for a change. Is that such a crime?"

Thud couldn't conceal his interest in the disagreement.

Thekla threw back her shoulders, determined to impress him. "You question my power, Lois? You want to see how powerful I am? Well, watch this. You're fired."

Lois was shocked. "You can't fire me."

"I just did."

"I want a recount," said Lois.

"Girls?" said Thekla. "Anybody care to comment?"

The other Tattletales looked horrified. In all the years of their club, no one had ever been fired before. They didn't know it was even possible. Everyone liked Lois, but if they stuck up for her, Thekla might fire *them*. It would be awful not to be in the Tattletales Club. So nobody spoke.

"Well," said Lois, blinking furiously, "you're all a bunch of losers." She turned and darted into the classroom.

Thud gave Thekla a thumbs-up sign. But Thekla suddenly didn't feel very good about what she'd done. She pretended she didn't notice Thud's approval.

By noontime, Professor Einfinger was in Vermont. He stopped at a barbershop in White River Junction. "Any recent lightning strikes in the neighborhood?" he asked.

The barber thought. "Well, old Miss Laurel Codliver's barn got struck last spring. Her station wagon got struck a week later. Then in the summer, she put up a garden umbrella over a picnic table, and it got struck, too. Burst into flames like a giant sunflower. Lightning just seems to love her."

"Any recent strikes?" pressed Einfinger. "Like this week?"

"Wouldn't know," said the barber. "She won't talk on the phone anymore nor even walk near a window. She's jinxed. If I were you, I wouldn't even go over to her house and ask her unless I was wearing a full-asbestos union suit."

Einfinger continued on to Woodstock, rented a room in the Woodstock Inn, and over dinner sat down to study the map some more and plan his campaign.

The next day, just before school was dismissed, Miss Earth said, "I'd like all of you to let me know how many sponsors you've signed up. Remember that a sponsor has to pay twenty-five cents for every egg you find, and that's a chunk of change. So don't be disappointed if your numbers aren't as high as you'd like."

Miss Earth wrote what she heard on the board. Thekla Mustard had the highest number of sponsors—eighteen.

"My dad has an ophthalmology practice and eyeglass store," said Thekla. "On the reading chart, he substituted the usual nonsense list of letters and instead made his customers read this sign." She held it up.

THEKLA IS GREAT.
SPONSOR THEKLA.
25 CENTS PER EGG.
DO IT FOR THE FIRE ENGINE FUND DRIVE.
IT'S A VERY NOBLE THING TO DO.
IF YOU CAN READ THIS, YOU DON'T NEED GLASSES.
BUY SOME ANYWAY AND START A FASHION TREND.

Thekla continued. "Many of his customers were happy to sponsor me. Even if I find only one egg, that's—let's see—that's four fifty right there. And if I come up with ten eggs, or twenty, well, I'd be raising forty-five to ninety dollars for the fund drive all by myself."

Most of the kids had signed up between five and ten sponsors. Hamlet wasn't a very large town. Pearl's sheet was empty, since she couldn't come. So was Thud's.

"Thud?" said Miss Earth. "Are you participating or not?"

"We'll see," said Thud in a noncommittal way. "Mom is nervous about going to Panama without me."

On Saturday morning at eleven o'clock, under the leadership of Sammy Grubb, the Copycats met on the porch of Clumpett's General Store. Hector, Mike, Salim, Forest Eugene, and Moshe. "We're only six Copycats today, since Stan is in New York state," said Sammy. "But we can still beat the Tattletales if we're systematic about it." He unfolded a large sheet of newsprint. He had drawn a grid over a map of the center of town, the area where the eggs would be hidden. "The hunt lasts from noon to one. I'm going to assign each of you guys a sector to scour. We'll put our eggs in a central location." He showed them a wicker laundry basket he'd borrowed from the display unit at Bucky's store. "Salim, you're going to be the guard and stand watch over this basket. We don't want any other kids, especially the Tattletales, stealing our hard-found eggs."

"I don't get to hunt?" asked Salim.

"Sorry," said Sammy. "But you've never done it before, and we can't take the time to train you. You'd run here and there like a chicken with its head cut off. Frankly, you're of more use to your brother Copycats as a guard."

"But I want to look for eggs myself *because* I've never done it before," said Salim.

"When it comes to being a Copycat," said Sammy Grubb, "you have to sacrifice your personal desires for the common good, which in this case is beating the girls."

"It's too bad, Salim," said Hector Yellow, "but it does make sense."

"Am I being discriminated against for being a foreigner?" said Salim. "Thud Tweed warned me about this."

"Next year you can hunt for eggs," said Sammy. "I'm sorry, but there it is."

Salim pouted. He'd told his parents and his baby sisters, Meena and Meera, about this exciting morning. They were going to come and watch. There'd be nothing to watch him do if he was just going to be standing next to a laundry basket. He could do that at home.

● ● ●

Across the green at the library steps, Thekla Mustard was conducting a pep rally with her Tattletale friends: Nina, Carly, Anna Maria, Fawn, and Sharday. Thekla began. "Now, my sister Tattletales, since I fired Lois out of the club, the numbers of the Copycats and the Tattletales are equal again, what with Stan's having left for New York state. It's going to be a close call. So in the interest of winning this contest, I authorize any dirty trick in the book."

"Why don't you tell Lois you're sorry?" asked Fawn in her usual small voice. "She would probably like to be a Tattletale again."

"I heard that!" shouted Lois, who just happened to be hanging out a few feet away, watching them. "I would not!"

"There's a bothersome racket in the air," said Thekla haughtily. "Girls, pay no attention. Sammy Grubb has been acting high and mighty lately. Let's show Hamlet who *rules* this town."

Ready to wreak charity, and woe betide all who got in their way, the girls went tramping over to the back of the town's pickup truck, where Mayor Timothy Grass was fumbling with a portable public address system.

The crowd gathered. Almost everyone was there. Even Old Man Fingerpie and his wife, Flossie, just back from their winter in Florida, had come down from their farm and were showing off their tans.

Ernie Latucci from WAAK had parked a van in front of Bucky Clumpett's store and was broadcasting his Saturday morning show live. He reported on the happy scene. "A lot of grownups lingering about, drinking coffee in paper cups and shivering, remembering the egg hunts years back when they were little and they did it for fun," said Ernie Latucci. "Today it's not for fun but for a fund drive. Kids are nicer today than we were."

"Oh, yeah?" muttered Lois, but her remark did not carry over the airwaves.

Mayor Grass said a welcome to everyone. Principal Buttle reminded everyone of the rules. The hunt would open officially when the first chime of the noon bells rang from the steeple of Saint Mary in the Tombstones. It would end when the chime rang the one-o'clock bell an hour later. Broken eggs would be discounted. "What a beautiful day for such an event, with a cloudless sky and the light so rich and pleasant," said Principal Buttle dreamily. "Children should feel grateful—"

BONG. The noon bell began to ring, interrupting her rhapsodies.

Pandemonium erupted on the village green. Most kids had made a mental note of the eggs they'd spied so far. They made a beeline to grab them. In the center of town, where there were bushes and stone walls, clots of damp leaves from the fall and heaps of last-chance snow, the eggs were well hidden.

Despite how eager the children were, a fair number of them paused long enough to notice a sleek Lincoln Town Car glide up to the front of the town garage.

The door opened. "Who could that be?" asked Ernie Latucci, his live show amplified all over the green. "Is it some government official come to observe the proceedings? If so, let's drum him out of office, folks, for ignoring the signs that say 'No vehicles allowed.' . . ."

All over the Upper Valley, devout fans of the Ernie

Latucci show heard a theatrical silence on the airwaves.

"Oh," said Ernie Latucci. "It's just some kid. What kind of kid in Vermont gets driven around in a ritzmobile?" He made some more jokes about it and then segued into Petunia Whiner's newest hit, "Baby Needs Burping."

> *"Ya got a little baby and your baby makes a mess.*
> *Dribbles on the carpet and vomits on your dress.*
> *Gets into your purse and finds your only set of keys.*
> *Throws them in the toilet. Should you murder Baby? Please.*
> * Just cuddle cuddle cuddle till the cows come home."*

It was a jaunty song, and Miss Earth, watching the proceedings, hummed along with it. Since she was not what you'd call gifted in the music department, a few birds on a nearby hedge flew away.

Thud Tweed hadn't expected to have his arrival announced over the AM radio station. He glowered. He went hulking across the green toward Clumpett's General Store, looking neither left nor right. "Hi, Thud," said Salim Bannerjee when Thud passed him loitering by the Copycats' wicker basket. Thud didn't answer.

He barreled into Clumpett's General Store and skulked around. Olympia Clumpett was standing at the register as usual, looking over the newest edition of the *Hamlet Holler*. "I see that the old Munning place has been sold," she said. "Wonder who has won Megadollars Sweeps and can afford that old plum of a place."

"I have," said Thud.

"Oh, have you?" said Olympia. "Well, then, you can pay for the candy that just accidentally dropped into your coat pocket. Or you can put it back on the shelf. Your choice. What's your family name again?"

"Tweed," said Thud, putting back a candy bar.

"What's your daddy do that brings in bacon with so much fat on it?"

"He's in the illegal purchase of body organs for donor transplant," said Thud. "He smuggles them into the country in ice-filled chests marked *XXX: Don't Open: Exposed Government Film Inside.*"

"That's a clever job," said Olympia. "Remind me to call him for a new stomach lining. I drink too much coffee, and my own stomach has more holes than Swiss cheese. Why aren't you out hunting the eggs with your friends?"

"Friends?" Thud laughed. "Them? They're ridiculous. You'd think they were six years old, running around like idiots."

"Well, they remind me what youthful vigor really means," said Olympia, rubbing the small of her back. "Tell you what. I may need a new spine and a new stomach, but my eyes are fine, thanks to my corrective lenses. You really want that candy so much, let's barter. Help me out. I haven't been able to get my hubby to clean up the motorcycle mess out back. You're a strapping big bruiser of a boy. Can you haul that wreck at least as far as the old icehouse? Stick it behind there? The weeds will grow up around it, and I won't mind it rusting back there if I don't have to look at it every day."

"Okay," said Thud, not so much to be helpful as to get the chance to examine the motorcycle again.

He headed out the back door.

On the green, Salim stood hunched over, glumly witnessing the fun of the egg hunt without being able to take part.

Lois Kennedy ambled by. She had only a few eggs in her

pocket. It was clear she was going not for numbers but for quality. "I got one painted like a dragon," she said. "See?"

"Neat," said Salim. "Is that a real dragon's egg you found?"

"Of course not," said Lois. "This is Vermont, not ancient Babylon. We elect Socialist representatives to Congress, not middleweight boxing champions. This isn't Cloud Cuckoo Land. And this isn't a dragon's egg, either. It's just a painted egg."

Salim said wistfully, "I can't hunt. I'm the guard. How are you Tattletales doing on your egg hunt? Is it fun?"

Lois reminded him that she wasn't a Tattletale anymore. "You should quit the Copycats," she said. "It's not too lonely, going solo."

Just then Salim's parents came over, dragging his twin sisters. Salim's slender mom wore a heavy tartan shawl and a Polartec fleece parka over her hot-pink sari. Salim's dad said, "So is it all the fun you hoped it would be, dear boy?"

"It's boring," said Salim. "I have to stand here and guard the eggs."

As he spoke, Hector Yellow and Forest Eugene Mopp came dashing across from the library, carrying seven eggs between them. They handed the eggs to Salim, panting, "More there! Back soon!" Away they raced.

"See?" said Salim. "No fun for me." Carefully he put the seven eggs in the basket, to join about thirty others already found.

"Why don't you hunt for eggs?" said Lois. "Your parents could guard the basket."

"I think it's not allowed," said Salim.

54

"Adults aren't allowed to hunt," said Lois. "But nobody said anything about them not guarding found eggs. After all, look, the adults by the truck are safeguarding the eggs their kids are bringing *them*."

"True, true," said Salim. He spoke urgently to his parents. They nodded, and Mrs. Bannerjee spread her shawl on the cold brown grass and sat down to make a lap for her babies to cuddle in. Mr. Bannerjee smiled and gestured for his beloved son to run along and find eggs and be a full-blooded American boy! With all the benefits of such!

"I haven't seen too many people over by Clumpett's," said Lois. "Want to look over there?"

"I suppose," said Salim. They ran to hunt in the bracken by the gas pumps. Then they meandered along the side of the store, poking around in last year's soggy weeds. When they turned the back corner of the building, they came across Thud Tweed and a heap of twisted motorcycle. Even after the rain, snow, and sunshine of the past three days, it was clear the motorbike had been roasted in a bonfire of some sort.

"Keep out—this is my turf," said Thud.

"What's that?" asked Salim. "It's an amazing place to hide some eggs."

"I'm not looking for eggs. What a baby game that is," said Thud. "I'm examining the wreckage for signs of foul play. The fouler the better. I think my father was involved. He's an undercover CIA agent."

"I thought he was a magazine publisher in Italy?" said Lois.

"I thought he ran a gambling casino in Calcutta?" said Salim.

"I thought you were going to Central America this weekend?" said Lois.

Thud shrugged. "Flight canceled," he said in a small voice. "Engine trouble."

"This is neat, but I don't see any other eggs here," said Salim. "Maybe I should go back to being a basket minder. I don't want to get in trouble with Sammy Grubb."

"You're a basket minder?" said Thud.

Salim explained. Thud looked interested. "Well," he suggested, "why don't you hunt for eggs in the dump behind the icehouse? That's where I'm supposed to haul this wreckage. Once I get it there, any eggs on the premises will be squished, so you should take your chance while you have it."

Lois and Salim hesitated. Was this a setup? They didn't trust Thud to steer them straight. But what harm could he possibly intend? It seemed rude to imagine real malice in him. So they disappeared behind the icehouse. Thud called, "I'll be right back. Don't go away." He lit out from the yard behind Clumpett's store, back out to the green.

Thud Tweed skidded to a stop. "Hello, Mr. Bannerjee," he said.

"Hello, fine young fellow," said Mr. Bannerjee, beaming.

"I'm a friend of Salim's. He asked me to come tell you something," said Thud. "He's found so many eggs that he doesn't need the ones in this wicker basket anymore. He said for you to give them to any girls in his class who come along. To be polite."

"Of course. Salim is a very polite boy," said his father.

"Nicest boy in Vermont *and* India," said his mother,

"which if you take the two populations together is probably over a billion people."

Thud pointed to Thekla Mustard, who was trotting nearby looking beady-eyed. "Here comes a girl who has found very few eggs. You could make her very happy."

"Salim would want it so," said Mr. Bannerjee. "Thank you so much for conveying his wishes to us, fine young fellow."

Thud took off before Thekla Mustard reached the Bannerjee family hovering over their wicker basket.

When Thud returned to the back of Clumpett's General Store, Lois and Salim were just emerging from the overgrown area behind the old icehouse. "Not a single egg there," said Lois glumly.

"Oh, well," said Thud. "Do you want to help me haul this metal carcass out of here?"

"Why should we?" said Lois.

"'Cause I'm the new kid in town, fragile and unsure of myself. A kind gesture might make me feel welcome and help me change my nasty ways," said Thud. "Also, I can beat you up, easy."

"I suppose he's right," said Salim. "He could."

"Yuck, my lovely trench coat will get dirty." But Lois grabbed a hold of a handlebar, Salim put his hands under the congealed slop of rubber from the melted tires, Thud put his big arms around the blackened innards of the engine, and on the count of three, they—*one-two-three*—heaved the thing out of its circle of ashes.

The rubber stuck to something and snapped, and the kids all fell backward.

"Hey, look," said Salim.

They peered closer. The rubber from the back tire seemed to have melted and congealed around something, making a protective casing. As the kids peeled the rubber back, they saw that the tire had taken the form of smooth cups, three perfect indentations the size of chicken eggs, like a rubberized carton.

"That's an odd place to hide Easter eggs," said Lois. "Boy, those grownups are good."

They crawled on their hands and knees. Sure enough, in the char and mess, three eggs, whole and entire, were nestled together. By some freak accident of luck, they hadn't been crushed. The tire had melted around them, molding a safe home for them for three days.

"They're still warm," said Thud, touching one.

9. Wanted, Dead or Alive

"Well, do these count?" said Salim.

"As what?" said Lois.

"As eggs for the hunt. They're not decorated like the others."

"Yes, they are," said Lois. "I mean—aren't they? Look."

The three kids leaned over even closer. At first glance the eggs seemed a sort of luminous beige. But when you looked closer, ghostly shadows seemed to be moving on the shells. A pulse of raw purple, a rush of pale rose. "These eggs are painted with a hand more talented than ours," said Salim solemnly.

"I don't know why they shouldn't count," said Lois. "I mean, we found them."

"I found them," said Thud.

"No," said Lois, "you found the motorcycle. We all found the eggs."

"Well, if I hadn't found the motorcycle, you wouldn't have seen the eggs, so they're mine," said Thud.

"If we hadn't helped you lift the motorcycle, you'd have crushed these eggs. So let's divide the booty. One for me"–she reached in and took one–"one for Salim"–she handed him the second–"and Thud, the last one is yours if you want it." She left it there.

"What would I want with a rotten egg?"

"It's not rotten," said Lois. "I think it's fertilized. I can feel movement in mine."

"I certainly don't want a pet," said Thud. "The word *sissy* doesn't begin to cover it."

"Well, I'll take it, then," said Salim. "If Lois isn't hunting eggs for the competition, and Thud doesn't want it, at least I can add this one to the Copycats' egg hoard." But as he reached for it, Thud's hand snatched it away. "I may not want it, but I want you to have it even less," he said. "Come on, help me move this motorcycle like you promised."

Softly, Lois and Salim set their eggs down by an over-turned wheelbarrow. Thud dropped his into his coat pocket. Lois and Salim winced, expecting to hear a crack. But good luck was with that egg. It held together.

Shifting the motorbike winded them, so they had no more breath to argue. When they were done, Lois and Salim collected their eggs and headed back to the egg hunt without so much as a goodbye to Thud.

"An egg is so neat," said Salim. "No edges, no rough-ness, no softness, no frills. No patterns within or without."

"Well, patterns within," said Lois, "if it's growing into a chick. All the genetic patterns, I mean, telling the chick how to grow into a chick and behave like a hen or a rooster rather than like–say–a lobster. Or a weasel."

"That's true," said Salim. "Can you feel how the weight

shifts as you hold it? As if some parts are heavier and other parts are lighter, and they're moving around."

"It's a well-formed chick inside, swimming in its private ocean," said Lois. "It thinks it has a perfect life in there. What a big surprise."

"It's even better out here, chickie," said Salim softly to his egg. "For one thing, you haven't got Miss Earth in there."

They had taken longer to move the motorbike than they'd realized. The egg hunt was almost over. Ernie Latucci was roaring over WAAK, the Voice of Vermont. "It's a great day to be alive! The eggs-citement on the Hamlet green is eggs-cruciating! We're eggs-actly seconds away from eggs-tracting the news about which class has won this eggs-traordinary eggs-ercise in egg hunting! And that's no yolk, folks! This is WAAK, the Voice of Vermont!"

Mayor Grass had a team of helpers to count and recount the piles of eggs gathered by kids from competing classrooms at the Josiah Fawcett Elementary School. Salim Bannerjee glanced around for his parents. When he couldn't find them at first, he looked for the wicker basket. It was over there at the feet of Principal Buttle, who was doing a second count for accuracy. He wove through the crowd and went and looked in.

"And the winner is," began Mayor Grass, "let's see, let me check the number—"

"Only seven?" Salim asked the principal. "Where'd all the other Copycats' eggs go?"

"Guess you really didn't need such a big basket," said Principal Buttle.

"With a grand total of *one hundred and nineteen eggs*, the

winner is the class of Miss Germaine Earth!" said Mayor Grass. Miss Earth tucked her chin into her scarf shyly and looked at the ground, but she clasped her hands over her head like a champion.

"Well, it's Miss Earth's class!" boomed Ernie Latucci. "Miss Germaine Earth, of Hamlet, Vermont! Look at the little lady! Folks, you should see the proud blush as she congratulates her students!" The girls were appearing through the crowd to rush up against her and scream with joy.

All except for Thekla Mustard, who was tugging at the coat of Mayor Grass and whispering something to him.

"Oh, a private competition," said Mayor Grass. He went back to the mike. "Folks, some late-breaking news. The winning class was holding its own private competition. The Tattletales Club, featuring the girls in Miss Earth's class, versus the Copycats Club, featuring the boys. I've been asked to announce the breakdown of Miss Earth's total. The Copycats found seven of the winning eggs. The Tattletales came up with the other *one hundred and twelve!*"

"Hurray for the Tattletales!" roared Ernie Latucci. "The girls trounce the boys! It could only happen here in Vermont, folks! Three cheers! Hip, hip—"

Salim looked wildly about. "There must be some mistake!" he said. "I demand a recount! We had *dozens* of eggs half an hour ago!" He spun around, catching sight of his parents emerging from Clumpett's General Store with cups of hot coffee clutched in their mittened hands.

But then Sammy Grubb walked up and stood close. Too close. Right in Salim's face. The other Copycats—Forest Eugene, Hector, Mike, and Moshe—ranged behind him like a wall of human concrete.

"What?" said Salim. "What happened? We've been hoodwinked."

"You left your post," said Sammy. "How could you let us down like that?"

"I found another egg to add to our number." Salim pulled out the new egg.

"Our poor pathetic number. The girls stole our eggs right out from under your nose, because your nose wasn't there to guard them."

"But I left my parents in charge—"

Sammy said, "What do they know? They never went to an egg hunt either. They handed eggs out right and left to any Tattletale who came begging. I caught your folks at it and yelled at them. But it was too late."

"You yelled at my *parents?*" said Salim. In India, children rarely yelled at adults. He was shocked.

"Now we're the laughingstock of the whole town," said Sammy Grubb. "The entire listening audience of WAAK, too. Salim, in all these years of my being Chief of the Copycats, I've never witnessed such a public drubbing."

Salim didn't know what to say. His mouth just hung open. Ernie Latucci was prattling on. All of Hamlet and an awful lot of Vermont and New Hampshire could hear him: "The Tattletales will rule the earth! The girls show us what boys are worth! At least in the classroom of Miss Earth!" The entire village of Hamlet was laughing.

"Well, at least we got eight eggs, not seven," said Salim in his smallest voice.

"At least you got eight eggs, not seven," echoed Thud Tweed nearby, in a nasty, mocking voice.

Sammy Grubb looked up sharply. Having Thud Tweed

witness the shame of the Copycats was suddenly too much to bear. He said to Salim, "You can keep your precious egg. No need to count it among ours. But let me tell you one thing, Salim Bannerjee. You'd better stay out of my path for a few days. You'd better lie low."

Sammy swaggered in a very Thud Tweedish manner.

Salim blinked back a sudden rush of hot wetness in his eyes. He turned and staggered and almost walked into a thorny leafless rosebush. His parents were coming up to him with huge, ignorant smiles on their faces. They'd had a great time. His vision blurred due to stinging tears, Salim could just make out Thud Tweed, off to one side. Grinning.

10. A Funny Story About Your Pet

On Sunday, Professor Einfinger followed leads in Woodstock, South Woodstock, and West Woodstock. He learned of a farmer who was said to have had a motorcycle recently struck by lightning. It took Einfinger nearly all day to track him down. It was nearly dusk when Farmer Ebenezer Rockefeller walked Einfinger out to a field behind his barn.

The motorcycle in question was a twelve-foot-tall modern art sculpture made entirely of imported beer cans. It hadn't been struck by lightning. It had been tipped over and trampled by the resident bull, who perhaps was irritated that all the beer cans were empty.

"Sell it to you for fifty," said Farmer Rockefeller.

"Fifty cents?"

"Fifty grand."

Einfinger declined and got back in his car. He checked his map. Quechee Gorge, Pomfret, Taftsville. Vermont sure had an awful lot of small towns.

● ● ●

When the school bell rang on Monday morning, Pearl Hotchkiss was the only student who behaved as if it were a normal day. She headed for her seat, whistling, slinging her lunch bag onto the shelf at the back of the room, calling out, "Hello, Kermit the Hermit!" to the class frog and "Hello, Miss Earth!" to the class teacher.

The Tattletales, walking in formation, marched in behind Thekla Mustard. Fawn, Carly, Anna Maria, Nina, and Sharday looked like cats that had swallowed a whole rainforest full of canaries. The girls took their seats, hugely pleased with themselves. "Isn't it great to be alive?" said Thekla. "At least, it is if you are *girls.*"

One by one, the Copycats straggled in without looking at one another or anyone else. Even Stan Tomaski, who had been out of town during the egg hunt, seemed gloomy. Sammy Grubb, who wasn't known to be troubled with a love of neatness, busied himself by arranging his pencils by order of size.

Salim Bannerjee slunk to his seat and dropped his head into his hands.

Thud Tweed was absent.

Lois Kennedy the Third was the last to arrive. She stomped in and took a good look around. "Something stinks in here," she said in a loud voice.

"I beg your pardon, Lois?" said Miss Earth, busy marking the attendance sheet.

"I'm going to apply to transfer to some other school."

The room grew quiet. "I don't know what you mean," said Miss Earth. "There isn't any other grade school in Hamlet, Lois."

"Maybe I'll ask for permission to be moved up a grade," said Lois, "or kept back a year. Starting today."

Miss Earth put down her pencil. "Something is wrong," she said softly.

"Something *is* wrong," snapped Lois. "Some of your students have no sense of honor, that's what's wrong."

"Is this so?" said Miss Earth, looking worried. She liked having honorable students. "Would you care to explain?"

"Those who are implicated in my remark *know who they are*," said Lois. "I have nothing more to add." She sat down. She'd been practicing her little speech on the bus all the way to school and was proud to have delivered it without flubbing. She glared at everyone.

"Well," said Miss Earth, "if there's nothing more to add, let's say the Pledge of Allegiance and begin the school day." The children stood and faced the American flag and made their daily promise. When they got to the final phrase, Lois Kennedy the Third was almost shouting "with liberty and JUSTICE for *ALL*."

"My, you feel strongly about the Pledge today," said Miss Earth.

Lois made no further comment. Thekla Mustard stood up. "With malice toward none and charity toward all," said Thekla, speaking to the whole room, "I'd like to commend *every one* of Miss Earth's students on the excellent job of egg-hunting we did. It allowed our class to contribute the most to the fund drive. In addition, I'd like to reward my loyal Tattletales." Thekla took some pink-and-white eggs out of her knapsack.

"On your own time, Thekla," said Miss Earth. "Remember, I don't like to spend class time on the clubs to which

67

you children seem bent on belonging. We have a lot of work to do today. Sit down, please."

Thekla sat down. But she had said her piece. She noticed with pleasure that Sammy Grubb and the boys were looking irritated. Good.

"One hundred and twelve to seven," said Thekla, *sotto voce*. "Pitiful."

"Thekla," warned Miss Earth, "I don't want to speak about the egg competition until we have all collected the promised funds from our sponsors. At that point we'll have a little classroom party to celebrate our win."

"The girls contributed the lion's share," murmured Thekla.

"It was rigged. Grand larceny. Fraud," mumbled Sammy Grubb.

"I'm being made the patsy," muttered Salim. "I'm taking the heat."

Lois didn't say anything, but she thought: Salim's dilemma is partly my fault. I was the one to suggest that his parents guard the eggs. How was I supposed to know they'd miss the point?

"Children!" said Miss Earth, "whatever you're whispering about, stop it. Now, I'd like to give you a creative-writing assignment this morning. Let's all write about our pets. If you don't have a pet, you can make one up. Write some way that your pet surprised you—"

The door opened. Thud came in, almost looking surprised at himself.

"You're late," said Miss Earth.

"Did I miss anything juicy?"

"Not yet. Please take your seat."

Miss Earth repeated the assignment. While the children got to work, Miss Earth calculated the total number of eggs found by her students times the number of sponsors paying twenty-five cents an egg. She was amazed at Thekla's haul: sixty-four eggs all by herself? At nineteen sponsors each paying sixteen dollars, Thekla alone would be bringing in three hundred and four dollars for the fire engine fund drive! Thekla's sponsors were going to be alarmed to learn what they owed, but the good folks of Hamlet kept their word. Grumbling about the high cost of eggs, no doubt, they'd all pay up.

When Miss Earth had finished, she could see why her class had won. In a single hour they had raised a little over a thousand dollars.

"Find a good stopping point, people," she said.

They put down their pencils. Miss Earth's class, by and large, loved creative writing. Arms went windmilling in the air for permission to read. Miss Earth looked around and saw the one person who wasn't volunteering. She said, "Why don't we hear from Thud this morning?"

"I don't like writing," said Thud.

"That's all right," said Miss Earth, smiling warmly. "We do. We like our writing and we like one another's. So read us what you have."

"Do I need to stand up?"

"No. From your seat is fine."

Thud stared at his sweaty paper as if finding it to be covered with text in Swedish or Sanskrit or Swahili. He sighed. "It's a sad story," he said at last.

"Go ahead," said Miss Earth. "It's Monday morning and the sun is shining. You'll find we're up for it."

Thud mumbled in an embarrassed voice, "Once upon a time there was a cat named Pussums and then it died. The end."

No one knew what to say. It was Thud's first academic effort so far, and they wanted to be encouraging. But it was hard to keep a straight face. First Sammy Grubb's mouth twitched, then Thekla Mustard's lips wriggled, then Pearl Hotchkiss took a little breath and you could hear a huge stack of laughs in her lungs ready to spill out. But if Thud Tweed knew they were laughing at him—well, that would be asking for a decapitation. Or worse.

Miss Earth sensed the roar of student laughter about to explode, and she intercepted it deftly. "Thud, I thought that was a fine start. It just needs a little—um—development."

"Don't be sad," said Thud. "It's a true story. I did have a cat named Pussums once. But it died. A Sears delivery van ran over it. I didn't care. I didn't like it."

"Let's do a peer edit. We can help you develop your ideas. Was it a boy cat or a girl cat?" asked Miss Earth.

"After the Sears truck got through with it, you couldn't tell anymore."

"Did it have any little tricks or unusual habits?"

"Once I left a bowl of cereal on the floor by mistake and Pussums used it as kitty litter."

"I think," said Miss Earth carefully, "I want you to do another draft of this story. Make us care that poor Pussums is dead by telling us what she—he—was like when alive. Can you do that?"

"*You* could do that," said Thud. "I never paid any attention to it. Probably it committed cat suicide."

"No," said Miss Earth, "I don't believe it."

70

"If someone snapped a mousetrap on *your* tail, *you* might run into the road, too—"

"STOP," said Miss Earth. "Let's go on to someone else. Let's see. Salim?"

Salim stood. Usually he was an enthusiastic contributor to the class and a great favorite. But today his color was gray and his voice monotonous. The bright spark in his eyes seemed cloaked. "I don't have a pet," he said. "My parents said it was a choice between a pair of gerbils and a pair of sisters, and we voted. I voted for gerbils, but they had two votes and they won and we got sisters instead. So my story is made up."

"Delightful," said Miss Earth, hoping it would be.

"I wrote about this egg I found Saturday," said Salim. He took it out of his pocket. "I imagined that there is a dragon in it. Here's my story."

Years of good student habits took over. He straightened his shoulders and read in his appealing voice with its formal accent.

"The Egg. Out of its hard brown shell, the dragon pokes her head. She has three little coils of red feathers on her scalp, and her wet wings are stuck to her sides, but with her beak she breaks the shell around her. She has been asleep in dragon water, but now she is awake. It's a mystery, but no more than any chick hatching from an egg is a mystery. Which came first, the chicken or the egg? Philosophers have debated this forever. I have the answer. The dragon came first, out of a magic egg. If you don't believe me, look at my egg. You can see the dragon inside, ready to be born." He held up his egg.

"Why, a show-and-tell story," said Miss Earth. "Marvelous."

"I have one, too," said Lois, not to be outdone. She took her egg out.

"Oooh," they said, as if a hen's egg were news.

"But those eggs must belong to someone," said Miss Earth. "Fertilized eggs wouldn't last outside a nest without a broody hen to raise them. Did you take them from someone's hen house?"

"They seem to have been abandoned," said Lois. "No hen in sight. Thud found one, too."

The other classmates all turned and looked at Thud. He shrugged. "I hit mine with a hammer and left the corpse out for the raccoons," he said.

The students gasped.

"Well," he said, "what do you expect of a guy who lets his cat get run over by a Sears truck? You want me to run an orphanage for baby chickies?"

"Oh, Thud," said Miss Earth, hardly believing her ears.

"An egg without a mother hen to raise it, what kind of life could it have?" said Thud. "I was just putting it out of its misery."

"We must find a hen to raise these other two eggs," said Miss Earth firmly.

11. Hiring a Hen

"Now, children," said Miss Earth, "this is Vermont, after all. Some of you must keep chickens and have room in your hen house for orphaned eggs? Hands, please?"

No hands flung themselves up.

"Vermont *has* changed," said Miss Earth. "I can't believe it. Nobody?"

"We have a dog," said Lois Kennedy the Third, "named Reebok."

"We have a cat," said Hector Yellow, "named Dogfood."

"We have a turtle," said Sharday Wren, "named Swifty."

"We have three fluffy white mice," said Forest Eugene Mopp, "named Cotton Candy, Cotton Wool, and Cotton Mather."

"We have a goldfish," said Nina Bueno, "named Stinky." Everyone looked at her and laughed. "Well, we always forget to change her water. She can't help it."

"We don't have any pets," said Carly Garfunkel, "but we have a flower left over from Christmas. We call it Loretta the Poinsettia."

"I get the picture," said Miss Earth hurriedly. When her children got started on their litanies, it was hard to stop them. "No one has a hen. Well, time marches on. Someone in town must still keep hens."

"I think Old Man Fingerpie does," said Lois. "When I walk past his place in the summer, I can hear them."

"I'll make a polite enquiry," said Miss Earth. "Thank you, Lois."

At noontime, when her kids gathered in the cafeteria under the watchful eye of Mrs. Brill, Miss Earth hurried to the nurse's office to use the phone. "You don't mind, do you?" she said to Nurse Pinky Crisp.

"Not at all," said Nurse Crisp. "I'm busy keeping up with whatever advances in pediatric health I can gleam from this *People* magazine."

Miss Earth looked up the number for Old Man Fingerpie and dialed it. "Hello? It's Miss Earth from the school. Hello! I'm talking to you on the phone." She put her hand on the mouthpiece and said to Nurse Crisp, "He's so old, he doesn't even remember that the phone was invented. He keeps thinking the handset is a kitchen implement for mashing potatoes with." She went back to the line and yelled, "It's Germaine Earth. *You* know. Grandma Earth's daughter. Grandma Sybilla Earth. I'm looking for a hen. I need to borrow a hen. I need to hire one."

Miss Earth listened, then screamed again. "I *know* you've been in Florida marlin fishing and drinking vodka all winter," she cried into the mouthpiece. "But you house your cows with Karl Rumpelmeyer while you're gone. Don't you do the same thing with your hens?"

There was a silence. Then Miss Earth's voice went down into a normal range. Flossie Fingerpie had taken the phone from her husband.

After she hung up, Miss Earth said to Nurse Crisp, "Flossie thinks the eggs my students found should be protected immediately. The Fingerpies will come over here with a hen to serve as a governess. If it's not one thing, it's another."

"Tell me about it," said Nurse Crisp. "I see here in this magazine that Petunia Whiner's got more personal heartache than the entire teenage population of Nashville."

"Gives her something to sing about, I guess," said Miss Earth.

As the children came back in from after-lunch recess, they heard the sound of an ancient pickup backfiring along the town green, taking Old Road to Crank's Corners toward the school. Old Man Fingerpie was a minor celebrity in town, since he had been born in 1899 and so his life spanned three different centuries so far. His wife, Flossie, would stage whisper behind his back, "He's supposed to be in the Great Beyond, but he keeps getting distracted by the Great Here-and-Now." She was a mere ninety-six and still had a few of her original teeth, which she was happy to show if you asked politely.

The two of them took about half an hour to get out of the cab of the truck. "This the school, ain't it?" Old Man Fingerpie kept booming. "Where's that sprog? Young Sybilla's little gal?" Principal Buttle met the Fingerpies and steered them slowly into the classroom.

Old Man Fingerpie had brought three hens with him. Flossie was carrying a paper sack, and she scattered seed corn at her feet every few moments. Most Vermont kids know hens, but to see a hen in a school is a special sight.

The first hen was black and elegant. She looked fluffed up, like someone just home from an appointment at the Hamlet House of Beauty. She ran from side to side. She kept crashing into the legs of Miss Earth's desk, and sometimes the legs of Miss Earth, too. "That's Minerva, Goddess of Wisdom, only she don't have much," said Flossie fondly. "We call her Nervy. She's a classic Buff Orpington."

The second hen was white with a few pale dove-gray markings. She stood perfectly still, like a contestant on a game show who couldn't believe she was about to blow her winnings on a simple question she couldn't remember the answer to, like "What is your name?" You never saw such a still hen. "That's a white Leghorn. We call her Lot's Wife," said Flossie, "because she looks mighty like a pillar of salt." She did.

The third hen was red. She had a cross-eyed, surprised look, as if she had just swallowed a Fourth of July sparkler. She pecked at her corn, trying to annihilate it by force of beak. "That's Medusa," said Flossie Fingerpie, "but we call her Doozy. Her breed is originally English. She's a Dorking."

"You can have your pick, but you cain't have all three," shouted Old Man Fingerpie. "One of them has a job laying breakfast eggs for us, and another one has an appointment to be chicken stew this Sunday. But you're welcome to the third, at least till your eggs hatch and your chicklings are fledged. Whaddya think?"

"Can we take the time to vote?" said Miss Earth.

"Take all the time you need. I'm aiming to live until my fourth century," said Old Man Fingerpie. He pretended to fall asleep on his feet, snoring persuasively.

"It's a joke," said Flossie. "But you'd better decide quickly, before he opens his eyes and forgets why we're here and changes his mind."

"I heard that," said Old Man Fingerpie in between snores. "It's terrible to be so old. I get in such a muddle. Watch out, or I might change my mind about you, Flossie. Seventy-five years is long enough to be married to one woman. I'll divorce you yet and marry this pretty little teacher."

Everyone laughed.

"Sorry, I've pledged my heart to another," said Miss Earth quickly.

Proof, at last, that she and Mayor Grass were engaged? Or was she only kidding?

It was a hard decision until Thud Tweed shook off his mantle of boredom and spoke. "Lot's Wife is too catatonic to do the work needed," he said. "And Nervy has got a couple of screws loose. Look at her." She was busy bashing her head into the side of the wastepaper basket. "Better vote for Doozy. She's mean, but she's got spunk."

As if to prove it, Doozy jumped right on Thud's arm and pecked it. "Ow," said Thud admiringly.

Doozy the Dorking won by a landslide.

"You take care of my little rooster, now," said Old Man Fingerpie.

"She's a hen," yelled Flossie into his hearing aid.

"I get in a muddle. I'm too old to concentrate!" he yelled back. "Let's go home, Marilyn Monroe!" But he winked at the children as Flossie escorted him out the door.

12. Doozy Dorking Adopts Some Eggs

Einfinger wandered into the public library in South Pomfret. A pleasant volunteer was tallying up receipts of the weekend's fundraiser book sale. "Passing through and looking for a good read?" she said. "Hardly anything left to buy. We had a huge turnout this weekend."

"You did?"

"Fourteen people and a dog. Bought out nearly our whole stock of donated books. Might be one left at the bottom of the box; I'll check in a minute. Look, we made nearly ten dollars."

"Anyone buy a book on eggs? Or biotechnology?"

"No. They mostly bought paperback novels by Stephanie Queen and self-help books. Do-it-yourself plumbing, wiring, psychoanalysis. That sort of thing."

It began to rain as Einfinger headed back to his car. The volunteer appeared again and caught him before he drove away. "Here's our only unsold book," she said. "It's an unauthorized paperback biography of Petunia Whiner. You can have it for fifty."

"Grand?"

"Cents."

He didn't care for country-western music. He drove away feeling depressed. To cheer himself up, he turned on the car radio and heard some dumb singer going:

"Ya got a little baby and ya got a lotta noise.
Ya gotta drop a bundle buying stupid baby toys. . . ."

He flipped the radio back off and turned the windshield wipers on.

The best student researcher in the class was Moshe Cohn. Since the school library could fit in one bookcase, Miss Earth gave Moshe permission to walk to town and ask Mr. Dewey, the town librarian, to help find out about the care and protection of poultry. Moshe came back with a stout volume called *The Chicken Book*. Its subtitle was *Being an Inquiry into the Rise and Fall, Use and Abuse, Triumph and Tragedy of Gallus Domesticus*. "This should do it," said Miss Earth. She began to do dramatic readings as the whim took her.

The children drew pictures of Doozy Dorking, who wandered up and down the aisles like a fashion model, examining her new surroundings.

"We need a hen house," said Miss Earth, eyeing the mess on the floor. "Our janitor is not going to be happy about Doozy's deposits. Let's see. This book says we'll require a hen run, seven feet of chicken wire, a roost, and a supply of water—besides the obvious chicken mash and straw and louse powder and the like. . . . I'm sure Principal Buttle is not going to approve of Doozy's setting up a residence here. Would anyone like to take Doozy as a houseguest?"

No one answered.

"It says here eggs gestate for about twenty-one days. Since these eggs are warm and there seems to be some movement within, I imagine it will take them only a few more days to hatch. What do you say?"

Nearly all the kids wanted to help. But they could imagine what their parents would say.

"Why don't *you* take him home?" asked Thud.

Miss Earth said, "My mother runs a bakery. In the eyes of the public, a chicken running around in a bakery is not a savory thing to imagine. Besides, since my mother also runs a car repair shop, Doozy Dorking would be at risk of getting run over by a motor vehicle. I'd hate to call up Old Man Fingerpie and give him the bad news about a dead chicken."

Doozy herself seemed distressed at the prospect.

Thud said, "The old icehouse behind Clumpett's General Store isn't being used. Maybe we could ask them to let us keep Doozy Dorking there until the eggs are hatched."

Everyone looked amazed that Thud had had such a good idea. Even Doozy looked amazed. But then she always looked amazed. She looked amazed to be alive at all, much less to be running around a classroom with everyone calling, "Here, Doozy-Doozy-Doozy" at her. She looked as if she liked the idea of a little privacy, a room of her own.

When the bell rang at the end of the school day, the children marched out the front door. The two town school buses were waiting. Since the rain had let up, some kids decided to walk home. Salim lived out Route 12 heading toward Forbush Corners. Lois lived on Squished Toad Road out beyond Old Man Fingerpie's farm. Being shunned by their respective clubs, Lois and Salim fell into step together as they headed toward the village green, after which their paths would diverge.

They didn't speak to each other for a while. Lois swallowed a few times and then remembered that she'd always claimed to be as brave as Thekla. Well, apologies took bravery. "I'm sorry about everyone being mad at you, Salim," said Lois. "It's partly my fault. But I never meant for you to get on the wrong side of the Copycats."

"Oh, who cares?" said Salim. "If they're so fickle, who needs them?" Lois thought she knew the answer to that question, but before she could decide whether or not to supply it, a car pulled up alongside them.

It was Thud's fancy car. The smoked-glass passenger window lowered with a soft, luxuriant purr. Thud stuck his head out the window. "Want a ride?" he asked.

Before either of them could answer, they heard a cluck from inside. Doozy Dorking was sitting on the black-leather seat next to Thud, complaining at the delay. "You're taking her to Clumpett's?" said Salim.

"Yes," said Thud. "Miss Earth thought that if she drove the hen there on her motorcycle, the hen's face might get blown off. So I volunteered to be the escort service."

Lois looked at Salim. He nodded. Salim knew what Lois was thinking. They probably shouldn't get into a fancy car without permission, but the future of their eggs was in jeopardy. So when Thud opened the door, Salim clambered in. Lois followed, as if she rode in style all the time so what was the big deal? She was especially happy to see Thekla Mustard staring at her jealously from the window of the school bus as it went past.

The passenger compartment smelled like the inside of a furniture store. The TV set mounted to a bracket wasn't turned on. "Reception is lousy in the mountains," said Thud, noticing their interest. "I could put on a CD if you want. We've got lots of Petunia Whiner CD's."

"Why bother?" said Lois. "Clumpett's is, like, four seconds away."

The Lincoln Continental coasted another few feet and pulled up in front of Clumpett's General Store. Salim said, "We've got our two eggs. You better take Doozy."

"I didn't really smash my egg. It's here in my pocket." Thud grabbed the hen under his arm. The hen clucked and struggled. "Tough it out, Doozy," said Thud, and slammed his way across the boards into the store.

"Well, lookee-see," said Bucky Clumpett. "It's the smilingest boy in town trying to squeeze all the air out of a pair of chicken lungs. I know this is Vermont, son, but you can't bring a chicken into this store. Not good practice when we're trying to sell food to the public."

"I need your help," said Thud in a voice that sounded as if he wasn't asking for help but demanding it.

"We conduct all conversations with fowl out the front door or the back," said Bucky. "Olympia, you okay to mind the till?"

"I hate to miss this one," said his wife, peering over the edge of her glasses. "I'm getting to like this lump of stranger here. Tell me what happens, Bucky."

"You bet, Limpy."

Olympia Clumpett watched her husband wander out the back door with the new kid in town and his straggling accomplices. Lois and Salim, wasn't it? Olympia didn't make an effort to know everybody's name, but if you run a store in a small town, it's hard to stay aloof.

When Bucky came back into the store, he was grinning. "We got tenants. We got ourselves a hen hotel on the property. Those three rascals are doing some sort of school project, so I struck a bargain. In exchange for cleaning out that old shack after the hen's confinement, they get to use it as a nursery."

"They don't exactly look like friends, those three," said Olympia.

"I called them rascals, not friends," said Bucky. "But give 'em time."

"In Vermont," said Olympia, "time is what we got." She drummed a pencil against her front teeth and looked at the town car hogging two spaces in front of the store, but decided to do nothing about it just now. Instead, she went back to the fascinating *People* magazine story about Petunia Whiner and her jailbird husband. The pictures were great. Outside the courthouse, he wore stripes, and she was holding a Kentucky Fried Chicken bucket up in front of her face to fend of the paparazzi. Ooh-la, the trials of the rich and famous. The hair, too.

13. The Hen Hotel

Tuesday lunch rush at Brooksie's in Sharon wasn't much of a rush. A salty old waitress rested against the counter and said, "Not that I've noticed one lately, but just why exactly *are* you looking for a motorcycle struck by lightning?"

"Oh," said Einfinger, "I don't know. The novelty of it."

"You want novelty, try our sun-dried watermelon chips with your salad."

"No thanks."

"A little garlic-and-salsaberry soda? It's a favorite of old-timers round here."

"I think not."

"How about the blue-plate special, creamed sardines on toast? Mighty tasty."

"Absolutely not."

"You flatlanders got no sense of adventure," she said, and went to chat with her other customer.

Miss Earth did not like being strict. She had to work up to it. But when the situation required it, she tried to rise to the occasion. She cleared her throat. "It's come to my attention that there have been some unpleasant goings-on in this room lately. Children being ganged up on, and excluded from clubs. I don't know the reasons why, but if it's true, I'm not impressed. Boys and girls, such behavior is precisely why I don't believe in clubs. The power of the mob can sometimes sway otherwise right-minded people into behaving like unthinking sheep."

The children sat in uneasy silence. Some of them folded their hands on their desktops like good children in TV shows dating from the olden days when everyone was impossibly good and boring.

"Miss Earth." Lois stood up. She spoke rapidly in a high voice. "Just in case anyone has the wrong idea, I want it to be a matter of public record that I am delighted to be cut free from the sheeplike mob of the Tattletales. If you've heard that I feel badly about it, you've heard wrong."

Salim added, "As for me, a membership in the Copycats Club was a good idea at first. It showed everyone that I was a regular guy. But now it's time to put such juvenile behavior behind me. I resign formally. I don't care to copy anyone."

No one believed a word of what Lois or Salim said. But Sammy Grubb looked sad, and Thekla looked annoyed.

"Moving on," said Miss Earth, who never lost an opportunity to teach, "we're going to do an impromptu unit on chickens and eggs."

Most of the class loved to do research. The school owned only one computer and usually the system was down. But today, due to some accident, it was up and running. When the kids arrived in the library, Mrs. Brill, the lunch lady, was busy making peanut-butter sandwiches at the checkout desk. "Be as quiet as you can," she said. "This is not a tomb, but it's not the playground, either."

The children broke into work pairs. Thud Tweed was coupled with Thekla Mustard. "You can do all the work," he told her.

"I usually do," she said sharply. "I'm good at this." She shoved Sammy Grubb and Pearl Hotchkiss out of the way and got to the terminal first.

While her students were engaged in research, Miss Earth nipped into the faculty lounge. Ms. Frazzle was there looking for an aspirin. Nurse Pinky Crisp was cleaning out the faculty fridge, exclaiming over various life forms growing in old pots of yogurt in the back. Jasper Stripe was changing buckets under a leak in the ceiling. Principal Buttle was working on the contracts for the following year. "I assume you're going to be with us still, Germaine?" said Hetty Buttle.

"Why ever wouldn't I?" said Miss Earth. "I love to teach."

"Rumor has it that you and Timothy Grass are seeing each other," said Hetty.

"Not on school days," said Miss Earth, a bit tartly.

"Ooooooooooh," said Ms. Frazzle. "A summer wedding! I'll do the flowers if you want."

"I'll play my banjo at church for you," said Jasper Stripe. "I can play Mendelsohn's Wedding March, complete with repeats, in under ninety seconds."

"I'll teach myself to sew over the spring break," said Principal Buttle. "Then I'll make your gown if you like. How hard can it be?"

"I would like some help," said Miss Earth. "I have a serious problem."

Her colleagues snapped to attention. "Sorry, Germaine," said Hetty Buttle. "What's the matter?"

"It's the new kid. Thaddeus Tweed. I think he's a bad influence. There's a lot more stress and strife among my students than usual. It's not just the boys against the girls and vice versa. Salim has resigned from the Copycats. Lois has been fired from the Tattletales."

"I should think you'd be pleased," said Ms. Frazzle. "You abhor the clubs, don't you?"

"I don't like the clubs, but I don't like it either when children are excluded from them. I'm worried that Thud is too worldly-wise for my children. Just too mean."

Principal Buttle shook her head. "No child is a bad apple. If I were you, Germaine, I would go over to that boy's house and request a parent-teacher conference whether the mother wants to spare the time or not. The child is too important to ignore. Where's the father, anyway?"

"Dead," said Miss Earth. "It explains a lot."

"Well, that's sad, but lots of children survive worse without becoming troublemakers or terrorists," said Principal Buttle.

"I think Thud has a serious lying habit, too," said Miss Earth. "I'll go see his mother again this afternoon."

When they all returned to the classroom, the children gave their reports.

"Male chicks are called cockerels, and female chicks are called pullets," said Fawn.

"Pullets start laying when they're six months old," said Sharday.

"The Dorking is a large, awkward, untidy bird of English origin. It has five toes and was introduced to England by Roman legions who liked chicken for supper," said Mike.

"Nobody knows how long chickens live, because most chickens are eaten either by foxes or by little old ladies from Crank's Corners," said Sammy Grubb.

"A hen can lay an egg every day or two," said Carly. "Some hens lay eggs all year long, but some stop for a Christmas break and don't start up again until about Easter."

"There's a breed called Auracana, or Easter egg chickens," said Moshe. "They can lay green or blue eggs."

"A chick needs warmth, mash, chick scratch, and water to survive," said Lois.

"Also a sanitary home environment," added Pearl.

"Chicks can die of pneumonia if they go out at night in the spring and it's too cold," said Anna Maria.

"Mr. Clumpett should sell a line of little chick parkas to prevent just such a disaster," suggested Forest Eugene.

"Chickens love dust baths. Exercise, sun, air, clean water, and a hobby, usually pecking at things. An old Christmas tree ornament suspended from the top of its cage, maybe," said Nina.

"A hen turns her eggs three times a day," said Hector. "A broody hen can get off her nest ten or twenty minutes a day and stretch her wings and forage for food."

"The average incubation for a chick," said Thekla Mustard, "is twenty-one days. Canny lovers of fowl know that a chick begins to scratch in its shell twenty-four hours before it is ready to hatch."

"Hens don't have eyelids," said Salim.

Stan said, "Mothers abandon their chicks when they get too large to sleep under her feathers at night."

"That's all very good," said Miss Earth. "Anything else? Thud?"

He had actually looked something up in an encyclopedia. He said, "The ancestors of chickens, and all birds, were the dinosaurs. So chickens have bloodthirsty blood in their veins. ROOOOOOAAAR."

After school, Miss Earth got on her Kawasaki 8000 Silver Eagle motorcycle and sped off to the old Munning estate.

While she had a shy streak, she still tried hard to do what was best for her students. And frankly, she didn't mind having a chance to get a look at the old Munning estate. "Lordy!" she said to herself at the sight of the house. "It looks like a parliament building for a rather prosperous midsize nation."

She rang the bell. The door was opened by a man holding a newspaper. She was flustered until she realized he was probably a butler. "I'm here to see Mrs. Tweed," she said.

He held the door open to allow her entrance. "Anything I can help you with?" he asked.

"It's official business," she said. "I'm from the Josiah Fawcett Elementary School."

"Very well. Please wait here." She was led to a side parlor decked out with gilt-edged mirrors and Oriental carpets. On a marble-topped table sat a copy of *People* magazine with a picture of Petunia Whiner on the cover. The caption read, "America's Songbird Sings Bitter Tune." Miss Earth loved Petunia Whiner's music, and her fingers itched to flip the pages and find out why America's Songbird was whining more than usual. But that might be rude.

"Miss Earth, I believe?" Mrs. Tweed appeared, looking unflappable and slightly annoyed. "So soon? I'd hoped you might handle things better than this. I'm quite busy, you know, and I detest getting mixed up in matters of scruff-and-tumble, as Thud's episodes inevitably become."

"How do you do?" said Miss Earth, remembering her manners. She almost curtseyed, as if Mrs. Tweed were a queen of some sort. It was that formal bearing, the regal set of the head. "I need to let you know how things are going after the first week, Mrs. Tweed."

"Better than you feared but worse than you'd like, I'll wager."

"Well—yes, as a matter of fact."

"Anything else you need to add?"

"Mrs. Tweed," said Miss Earth, "Thud has said you are in poor health and require constant transfusions in Panama. I'm concerned for your welfare as well as his."

"Miss Earth," said Mrs. Tweed, "I am a very private person. I'm not inclined to answer your questions about my well-being. Has Thaddeus wounded any little children or caused an unreasonable amount of damage to the fabric of the school building?"

"No." Miss Earth felt compelled to add, "Not yet, anyway."

"Good. When he does, handle it, please. Is there anything else before I show you to the door?"

"Mrs. Tweed," said Miss Earth, "as a teacher, I expect that parents will make an effort to take some small part in their children's education. To display some interest. Even to show up in school once in a while. Couldn't you give your chauffeur a day off every now and then and drive Thud–I mean Thaddeus–to school yourself? He might be a little less ornery if he thought you cared."

For an instant Mrs. Tweed looked hurt, as if it were just possible that she cared a great deal. But some habit of self-control got the better of her. Her expression resolved into its usual polite ferocity. Crisply, she said, "I'll apply for a driver's license at once. Miss Earth, don't presume to tell me about my son. He's a chronic liar, so you waste your time trusting what he says. And now, if you'll excuse me? Harold, please show Miss Earth to the door. Then lock it."

Why do I feel like an unwelcome door-to-door sales-woman? thought Miss Earth. I'm a *teacher*. I'm just doing my *job*.

At the same time, Lois, Salim, and Thud were hanging out behind Clumpett's store. They spent about an hour with Doozy Dorking, making sure she was happy. She was sitting on the eggs, which she already thought of as hers, and she didn't like the children to get too close. Salim had brought some Indian decorations. Black and purple hangings featured pictures of magical beasts stitched in silver sequins. Red fringe swayed as Doozy Dorking strutted past. She liked to nip at the fringe.

Lois had made a sign with felt-tip pens. In jaunty letters it said:

The Hen Hotel

She hung it up on a couple of rusty nails over the door. "I like it," said Thud. "You know why?"

Neither Lois nor Salim answered, but they looked en-quiringly at Thud.

"My dad is in the Witness Protection Program, and it's safe for him to come to see us only if we move constantly. That's the real reason he's not living here with us. I've spent most of my life moving from place to place, from hotel to hotel, so when he does pay us a secret visit, no one suspects it."

"Well, you're one of the managers of the Hen Hotel," said Salim firmly. "Don't plan on moving anytime soon. You have your chick to take care of when Doozy goes into retire-ment."

"I'll take care of her all right," said Thud. "Just you watch."

Neither Lois nor Salim liked the sound of Thud's voice. But what could they do? The sun felt good on their shoul-ders. Doozy looked dozy. With luck, Thud was all talk and no action. They just stood and watched the hen carefully keeping those eggs warm.

Then they heard the first little scratchy sound of a chick pecking the inside of the shell. And they knew. If what Thekla had reported that day was correct, the first chick would begin to hatch within twenty-four hours. The kids were filled with delight. Even Thud had to work to keep his face from appearing thrilled.

14. Knock, Knock. Who's There?

On Wednesday, following a lead, Einfinger visited an art gallery in Norwich. Some local photographer was showing luridly colored pictures of lightning striking telephone poles, oak trees, church steeples, and, in one lucky shot, a very shocked-looking cow.

"These are great," Einfinger told the curator. "But no motorcycles?"

"She does it all by computer graphics. She could zap a motorcycle for you if you wanted. Twenty-four-hour turn-around. Here's our card."

"No thanks," said Einfinger. "I want the real McCoy, not a simulation."

Schooldays on Wednesdays always seemed to last the longest. Today more than usual. Even Miss Earth's best teaching manner, full of zest and kindliness, wasn't enough to keep Lois, Salim, or Thud engaged. They kept sneaking sidelong glances at each other and grinning.

Sammy Grubb couldn't help but notice. This was an odd development.

Thekla Mustard was also curious. As far as Thekla was concerned, Lois Kennedy the Third was a loose cannon. Sooner or later she'd have to be dealt with.

After recess, Miss Earth said, "Well, now, let's turn to Free Reading. Everyone have a book?" asked Miss Earth.

No one answered her.

"Do you have a book, Thaddeus?" asked Miss Earth.

"No."

"Well," said Miss Earth, "does anyone have an extra book Thaddeus can borrow?"

"He can look on with me," said Fawn Petros in her little mouse voice. Fawn preferred picture books to novels. She was rereading an old Dr. Seuss favorite, *Horton Hatches the Egg*, in which an elephant sits on an egg and is rewarded for his pains by hatching a chick that's part bird, part elephant. It was probably not a true story, but Fawn liked the pictures. Thud scraped his desk noisily across the floor toward her. Fawn flinched but held her ground. Thud grabbed the book and tugged it onto his desktop.

"Ha! Ha! Look at that huge pachyderm balancing on an egg!" cawed Thud.

"This is quiet reading time," said Miss Earth in a mild voice.

"Yeah, but this is really great stuff," said Thud.

"We know," said Miss Earth.

"I never saw this piece of propaganda before," said Thud. "Talk about your alternative families."

"Thaddeus," said Miss Earth in a warning way.

"Yes?" asked Thud.

"She means," said Thekla Mustard witheringly, "shut the thud up."

At lunchtime the children raced into the cafeteria. Mrs. Brill supervised their arrival with her usual expression of high dudgeon. The children greeted her with high spirits. They loved lunch.

Thekla Mustard gathered the rest of the Tattletales at a table. They sat shoulder to shoulder, blocking out sight of other kids. "It's my opinion," said Thekla, "that Thud, Lois, and Salim are on the verge of forming their own club."

"So what?" said Nina. "No one says we have to stay a two-party system. The more the merrier, I think."

"I worry for poor Lois," said Thekla. "She appears feisty, but I think deep down she's suffering. Perhaps we should invite her back to join us. For her own well-being, not to mention protection."

"Thekla," said Carly, "you're just peeved that someone else has a life. Don't worry. We're still the best club in the classroom. I miss Lois, and I wish she'd come back, but I don't think she needs our help all that much. She's stronger than you give her credit for."

"Maybe so." Thekla shrugged her shoulders. "But I still think Thud is a bad influence. I think Lois is going to go over to the dark side. I hope it doesn't happen, but I've *done my best*." She bit healthily into her radish-and-raisin sandwich.

Across the room the Copycats were having a similar conversation. "Do you think we should ask Salim to rejoin us?" asked Hector.

"We never kicked him out," said Sammy Grubb. "He left of his own accord. He can sit with us anytime he wants. It's a free country." Sammy meant this. He missed Salim, and he was sorry to have lost his temper. But sometimes when a disaster between friends starts to roll in a certain direction, it's hard to stop it.

Sammy glanced around for Salim and found him sitting at a far table with Lois and Thud. Sammy had his hand all ready to wave Salim over to the Copycats' table. But Salim's head was bowed. He was deep in conversation with Thud and Lois. Sammy couldn't get his attention.

Sammy sighed and, for consolation, licked the frosting off a cupcake. Then he balled up the leftover cake part, squished it into a patty, wrapped it carefully in a candy wrapper, and handed it to Thekla Mustard on his way out to recess. "A present, Thekla," he said.

"Thanks, Sammy," she answered, "but I'm allergic to anything you might give me." She threw it away without opening it.

"I can't believe we're doing this," said Salim. "In all my days at grammar school in Bombay, I never did anything this bad. Ever."

"This isn't so bad," said Lois. "It's against the rules, but no one's getting hurt."

Thud said, "You kids all act as if you're trying to win some kind of award for childhood saintliness. We're just playing hooky for half an hour. That's all."

Avoiding the road, the three kids were roaming across the wet fields and over the stream that separated the school-yard from the village green. It was only a ten-minute bushwhack from the Josiah Fawcett Elementary School to the center of Hamlet.

The kids kept behind stands of bush where they could. But there was no way to get across the center of Hamlet without being seen. So Thud said, "Just straighten up, and if anyone asks, we're going to the library to do some more research on chickens. The way Moshe did the other day."

As they crossed the green, a car came along and tooted its horn at them. "Oh, beloved stars of morning," said Salim, panicking, "it's my mom!"

Mrs. Bannerjee was pulling her car over to the verge. She rolled down the window. "Salim-ba!" she shouted. "What are you doing away from the school?"

"Hello, Mama," said Salim. He had never lied to his mother in his life and he did not know how. "These are my friends, Lois and Thud."

"Hello, Miss Lois," said his mother, "and very nice to see you again, Master Thud. But Salim, you have not answered my question."

"We're on our way to the library, Mrs. B," said Thud. "We have an important school assignment to do."

"Why aren't you at work?" asked Salim weakly.

"I had an eye appointment with Dr. Mustard," said Mrs. Bannerjee. "I am going in just now. What is your assignment about?"

Salim just stood with his mouth open. He couldn't say a thing.

"We're doing research on mythology," said Lois, coming to the rescue. "We're trying to find out if there's any creature in folklore that is part chicken and part elephant."

"You mean besides the little bird thing in *Horton Hatches*

the Egg?" asked Mrs. Bannerjee. "I can't think of one. Let me know what you find out, Salim. Goodbye, children!" She sped off to her job at the Locust Computer Labs in Hanover, New Hampshire.

"Hoooh, boy, that was close," said Salim. He was sweating.

"We have our chicks to look in on," said Thud. "What's a little lie when it's in the service of baby chicks?"

But Salim didn't like the way he felt. How easily his mother had believed their alibi! And why not? She'd trusted her darling son his whole life long.

And when had his mother met Thud Tweed before?

They weren't a moment too soon.

Doozy Dorking had backed away from the nest. She was looking worried. When Thud, Lois, and Salim crept into the Hen Hotel, she didn't even fuss at them. She just stared at the biggest egg.

What was that sound? The kids knew it from old movies. A sound like an old-fashioned typewriter, someone pressing one key at a time, over and over. Peck peck peck peck. The egg wobbled a bit and a crack appeared. Peck peck peck.

"Look," said Salim.

"Oh, the wonders of nature!" said Lois, feeling that Miss Earth would love to witness this.

"Cool," said Thud. "The very first act of its life, and it's a destructive one. Here it comes!"

A tiny bit of shell about the size of an aspirin jettisoned up, eighteen inches in the air. A beak showed itself.

"It looks like the fin of a tiny shark!" breathed Lois.

98

The beak rubbed itself against the shell, widening the cracks. Then it managed to grip the shell like a nutcracker. It broke off a bit and tossed it away, and broke off some more.

"Who are you?" said Salim.

"Welcome to the world!" said Lois.

"You are one bad little critter!" said Thud.

The head popped out. It swiveled around and looked at them.

"Awwwwwww!" said Salim. "I love it!"

"Awwwwwww!" said Lois. "I love it!"

"Awwwwwww-ful funny-looking chick," said Thud.

The chick looked as if it had had a shampoo and had not yet rinsed off the suds. Its yellowy fuzz was damp and lathery. It had a funny little greenish topknot of several uncoiling feathers. It blinked its eyes.

"That's odd," said Salim. "Did I just see it blink? I thought hens didn't have eyelids."

It blinked again as if to prove that it could.

Then it opened its little beak and emitted a small jet of fire, about as strong as a cigarette lighter's flame.

15. The ABC's of Hatching Chicks

"**M**y crab cakes at lunch must have had too much curry powder in them," said Salim. "I'm seeing things."

"I saw that, too," said Lois. "I can't believe it. It's a freak of nature!"

"A little vandal!" said Thud admiringly. "Look! An arsonist! Hey, chick, aren't you too young to be smoking already?"

The chick looked both bleary and astounded. Well, maybe all newborn things looked that way. It twisted its neck and studied the rest of the egg in which its body was encased. "Hey, want some help there?" asked Thud, and leaned forward to break the eggshell. But Doozy Dorking rushed at him, squawking and flapping her wings, and she pecked him on the arm so hard that she drew blood.

"I think it's probably good for the chick to get itself out," said Lois. "A little aerobic exercise."

The chick was hard at work, struggling and pecking and

squirming and kicking. It muscled its way out. Some gluey glop spilled, a bit of the bathwater in which the chick had been floating. And then at last it was out, poking and shaking itself, practicing its balance, taking a small step or two and then pausing for breath. It was exhausted.

Doozy Dorking stood nearby and looked at it. She clucked a few times hopefully. The chick looked up at her and emitted a small cheep. Doozy fluttered with relief and waddled outside, on the hunt for seed corn or bugs, as if to teach the chick what to do. The chick wobbled uncertainly after her. It came to a bit of corn and opened its mouth. It shot out that little jet of flame again. The kernel exploded into a bit of popcorn. The chick fell down on its bum.

Doozy came over, took the popcorn, and flung it into the bushes.

"What the blazes is *wrong* with that chickie?" said Salim. "It's got a very special case of bad breath."

"Poor thing," said Lois.

"Lucky thing," said Thud. "That's *my* chick, you know."

"How do you know?" said Lois.

"It came out of my egg. My egg was on the top. It was the biggest. Didn't you see it?"

"The eggs all look the same to me," said Lois.

"Me, too," said Salim.

"Well, too bad," said Thud. "That's my chick. I can tell. Doesn't its little feather cap look like an alien hairpiece?"

They were so enraptured by the sight of the chick running after Doozy Dorking that they didn't hear the back door of Clumpett's General Store open. "Whaddya know," said a voice. They turned. It was Bucky Clumpett. He had a pile of old newspapers he was stacking up in an orange crate for recycling on Saturday. He put them down and came over. "Looks like your Hen Hotel has a baby customer. Hey, chick-chick-chick-chick."

The chick didn't pay any attention to Bucky. The kids hoped that it wouldn't breathe fire while Bucky was looking. He might refuse to let it stay in the Hen Hotel. "How are the other ones doing?" asked Bucky. "When you get one chick, you often get the others. I think they hear each other and they don't want to be left out of the party."

"Everyone's still asleep in there," said Salim. "But it won't be long, I bet."

"Mighty cute, aren't they?" said Bucky.

"Bucky!" called his wife. "That trooper from the state police is here to talk to you! He's got a bee in his bonnet about something."

"Coming, Limpy," he answered. "You kids, watch that chick. Make sure it doesn't get out of the chicken wire. I bet some old fox would enjoy that particular chicken nugget."

"I pity the fox that tries," murmured Lois, but too low for Bucky to hear. He turned and clumped inside.

"I wonder how strong that flame is?" said Thud. "Do you think it could burn down the Hen Hotel? We better do an experiment and find out." He grabbed the top newspaper from the stack of recycling and went toward the chick with it. "Come on, chickie, light my fire," he said.

"I'm not sure you should give it any ideas," said Salim. "It's a sensitive little soul."

"Welcome to the wide world of juvenile delinquency," said Thud. He held out the front page. The chick opened its beak to take a bite. A tiny fingerlet of flame flickered out and singed the edge of the paper, but it didn't light fully. "Well," said Thud, "it's not likely to become an arsonist and burn down the Hen Hotel, let alone run amok in the streets of Hamlet setting the whole town on fire. Darn."

"I think I'm glad," said Lois, "but I'm not convinced we're out of the woods yet."

"We'd better head back," said Salim. He picked up the paper to return it to the bin. Then he said, "Hello. What's this?"

He held up the front page of yesterday's *Boston Globe*. A headline at the bottom of the page had caught his eye. It was a feature article. Salim read the story aloud.

MOTHER NATURE'S AVENGERS CLAIM: SCRAMBLED EGGS ARE POACHED!

(Special to the *Boston Globe*)

The highly secretive biotech sabotage league Mother Nature's Avengers has issued a statement called "Fowl Play!"

The statement avers that a Boston-area biotech firm, Geneworks, has been secretly developing a variety of poultry from chicken cells spliced with nucleic material derived from the genetic material of a foreign species. Mother Nature's Avengers suspects the fertilized eggs feature snips of DNA from the rare blue-toe lizard found only in the Galápagos Islands. In part, the nine-page manifesto reads:

> A highly placed mole in Geneworks, Inc., in Waltham, Massachusetts, reported the removal

from their incubator of seven fertilized hen's eggs that had been "doctored" for genetic mutation. Packed in a thermally sensitive carrying case, the eggs were en route to Dartmouth College for prenatal inspection by a chicken doctor on the faculty. Mother Nature's Avengers intercepted the eggs. Subsequently they were destroyed by a freak bolt of lightning.

Mother Nature's Avengers regrets the loss of life and limb to the unborn, genetically freakish chickens. However, we propose that even Mother Nature herself is alarmed at the extent to which unscrupulous biotech firms such as Geneworks are trying to do the work of Dr. Frankenstein and originate new species through stewing respectably evolved genes in a kind of primordial-ooze genetic brew.

The *Globe* has been unable to confirm or deny reports of the existence of genetically altered chicken eggs or their subsequent theft and demise.

The *Globe* has also been unable to reach anyone from Geneworks for comment. A sign taped to the front door reads, "Closed for renovation," though a staff of several hundred can be seen coming and going at all hours of the day and night. The principal shareholder and CEO of Geneworks is Dr. Protestina Elderthumb, long considered a front-runner for the Nobel Prize for Cellular Biology until she gave an inflammatory lec-

ture on designer genes at the 1992 World
Congress of Geneticists in Oslo, Norway.

"I don't get it," said Salim. "Are these chicks from *those*
eggs? Are they chickie-lizards? And if this is all over the
news, then the Clumpetts know about it. They'll tell that
state trooper or whoever is in there right now what is hatching in their old icehouse."

"Maybe," said Thud.

"Or maybe not," said Lois thoughtfully. "Remember—
the Clumpetts don't know that these eggs were found here.
They were busy watching the store during Saturday's egg
hunt. They didn't see us back here. Even if they read this article and guessed that this motorcycle was carrying genetically engineered chicken eggs, they think *those* eggs are history. Let's just keep quiet about it."

Doozy Dorking lifted her head. She went hurrying back
into the Hen Hotel, the new chick bouncing and staggering
along behind her. "She's heard another egg cracking!" said
Salim. "And so do I!"

It was not one egg but two. The other two little chicks were
beginning to emerge. Each one had a tiny green tuft of feathery
business at the top of its crown. They looked identical.

Lois ran into the store to ask for a little snips of colored
yarn to tie around the leg of each little chick. Red for
Thud's, blue for Salim's, yellow for Lois's. She heard Bucky
Clumpett saying to the state trooper, "Well, the facts of that
Globe story sure do match. And if you want to examine the
motorcycle again and see if it's still got egginess stuck to it,
be my guest. But didn't you say that Einfinger fella said he'd
already found his stolen briefcase?"

Lois grabbed the yarn and raced back outside. Without pausing to tell the others what she was doing, she hurried to the heap of motorcycle wreckage. She found the bit of congealed rubber that had cradled the three undamaged eggs. Proof of their possible survival . . . She managed to tear off that hank of rubber, and she flung it into the woods.

Then, despite Doozy Dorking's protests, the kids scooped up their chicks and tied yarn around their ankles. "I think I'm going to call mine Flameburper," said Thud.

"They *all* burp flame . . . look," said Salim. "But I don't think we can give them names yet till we know what they're like."

"For the time being," said Thud, "they can be called Flameburper A, B, and C. Mine is A, though."

"Mine will be B," said Lois.

Salim had no time to complain. Across the green they could hear Mrs. Brill ringing the bell to signal the end of lunch. They put Flameburpers A, B, and C back in the Hen Hotel with Doozy Dorking. Then Thud, Lois, and Salim hurried back to the Josiah Fawcett Elementary School. They hoped that even if Trooper Crawdad came out and poked around the motorcycle, and even if he did see the hen and the chicks, he wouldn't guess who the three newly hatched chicks were.

Their hopes were largely realized. As Trooper Crawdad examined the motorcycle and the remains of the metal briefcase, the cooing sounds Doozy made were drowned out by the noise of the nearby stream rushing with spring runoff. Trooper Crawdad never noticed a thing.

"This sure seems like the motorcycle I read about in the

newspaper. Poor little destroyed chickies," said Trooper Crawdad. He was as partial to a nice deep-fried drumstick as the next fellow, but he still felt sorry for the devastated eggs. "But if so, I wonder why that Professor Einfinger claimed he had found his suitcase. And could it be possible that freak chickies are vital to our nation's security?"

16. The Boss
of the Rotten Eggs

Lois was distracted. She kept imagining the Flameburpers accidentally burning down the Hen Hotel.

Salim was distracted. He kept feeling ashamed at having stood by as his friends lied to his mother.

Thud was distracted. He felt like a changed boy. He was a new creature. He was no longer a thug with a heart like a time bomb. He was in love.

Yes, he was in love. Thud Tweed was in love with a baby chick.

Flameburper A. The one with the red yarn around its right leg. It was so cute! Thud couldn't stand it. He had never really had a cat named Pussums. That was all lies. He'd never had a pet at all. He had never stayed in one place long enough to get one. But A was perfect. Its little green tuft up top was almost like a Mohawk. Thud loved A's funny little inflammable breath. And how it chased after Doozy Dorking! Running, falling, bumping into Doozy's big feathery rear end. Flameburper! *Flameburper A!* If it turned out to be a pullet, he could call it Amy. If a rooster, Amos. A! The first, the best, the only! A—numero uno!

"Thud, are you paying attention?" said Miss Earth.

"No," said Thud.

"Well, at least you're telling the truth," said Miss Earth. "Would you like to pay attention?"

"No," said Thud.

"That's too much truth for one day," said Miss Earth. "This might be the time for a harmless little white lie, Thud. Give me a different answer."

"I'll be happy to pay attention for the rest of the day, Miss Earth," said Thud.

It was the first time Thud had actually addressed her by her title. The other kids in the class noticed. Hmm.

Miss Earth thought she could guess why Thud was so distracted. "You're worried about those eggs hatching while you're in school, aren't you?" she said. "Well, don't worry, Thud. Doozy Dorking is a capable hen. She'll take care of the chicks if they hatch while you're at your schoolwork."

"Yes, Miss Earth," said Thud.

"You'll let us know as soon as they're born, I'm sure," said Miss Earth.

"Of course, Miss Earth," said Thud. For the first time ever, Thud thought a lie might actually be permissible. Those little freak chickies needed protection from the outside world. And he'd lie and cheat and steal in their defense. He'd rip the face off any geeky scientist coming to reclaim them from Geneworks, Inc., or Dartmouth College or anyplace else. He'd wrestle any known Copycat or Tattletale into the mud who tried to get between him and Flameburper A. Or B or C, for that matter.

● ● ●

After school, Lois, Salim, and Thud raced back to the Hen Hotel. Bucky and Limpy Clumpett were too busy unpacking a shipment of denim work clothes to pay much attention. "I can hear the little chorus of cheeps out there. Happy birthday! Male or female?"called Limpy, her head deep in a cardboard carton as she hauled up the last of the Fatboy Overalls. "You can tell by holding them upside down. Males can bend and try to peck your fingers. Females can't."

The Hen Hotel was still standing. It had not burned to the ground. Maybe the chicks were already learning how to govern their bad breath. Except for the greenish tufts sproinging in a sprightly fashion out of their heads, the chicks looked pretty ordinary. Doozy Dorking was lovingly ignoring them, eating up every bug that appealed to her. The chicks raced after her. They twirled in circles like windup toys. They fell down and got up again. It took Thud, Lois, and Salim a while to snatch up their chicks. They took turns testing to find out the genders.

A was a boy. "Amos," said Thud. "A little bruiser! He's trying to bite me."

B was a girl. "Beatrice," said Lois. "She's so *funny!* She's crossing her eyes at me to make me laugh."

C was another boy. "Seymour," said Salim. "Because he's always looking around and seeing more."

Amos, Beatrice, and Seymour: the Flameburper triplets.

"You've been holding out on us!" said a voice.

They turned. Thekla Mustard and Sammy Grubb were standing at the corner of the back yard of Clumpett's General Store. Amos, Beatrice, and Seymour all ran into the Hen Hotel to hide.

"Thekla Mustard and Sammy Grubb! Together at last!" said Lois. "Never thought I'd see the day! What brings you out walking together like a pair of lovebirds?"

"Cut it out, Lois," snapped Thekla, glaring menacingly. "Do you think we can't smell a rat? Clearly something's been going on, and we decided to find out what. These chicks are hatched! They're here! Why didn't you tell us? As Empress of the Tattletales, I have the right to know."

"You fired me from the Tattletales, remember?" said Lois.

"Hey, Salim," said Sammy. "I didn't fire you from the Copycats."

"No," said Salim. "I've put myself on permanent leave."

"Well, you can take yourself off it if you want," said Sammy Grubb. "You're always welcome back, you know. You're an important part of the Copycats."

There was a silence. Before Sammy could think of what to say, Thud Tweed spoke up.

"Hey, Grubb," he said. "We got our *own* club. As of right now. We're not Copycats. We're not Tattletales. We're the Three Rotten Eggs. And Bannerjee's a Rotten Egg now. And I'm the boss. So lay off and shut up."

Salim and Lois both glanced at Thud. They hadn't discussed any of this. They'd never formed a club called the Rotten Eggs. They certainly hadn't elected Thud the leader. And while they didn't like Thekla and Sammy nosing into their business and spying on them, they also didn't like Thud saying "shut up" to Sammy.

"Boss of the Three Rotten Eggs," Thud repeated. "I like the sound of that. Hey, Flameburpers, you hear that? I'm the Boss!"

Amos came running out of the Hen Hotel. He fell off the little ramp onto his beak and cheeped in dismay.

Beatrice came running out to see what happened and fell on top of Amos.

Seymour followed and began to tug the others to their feet. When Beatrice was righted, she did a little victory dance, a kind of poultry polka. But when Seymour went back to help Amos, Amos blatted out a little gust of flame at him. Seymour backed up and cheeped in surprise.

"What was *that?*" asked Thekla Mustard.

"Nothing," said Lois quickly.

"That was not nothing," said Thekla. "My father is an ophthalmologist, Lois, and with my corrective lenses I have the best vision in Hamlet. I just saw that chick make a fiery remark. What is going on here?"

"Visiting hours are over," said Thud. "The Boss of the Three Rotten Eggs has spoken." He raised his fist. Thekla and Sammy glanced at each other and backed away.

17. Wooing the Renegades Back

From Thetford Hill, Einfinger put in a call to Dr. Elderthumb.

She was apoplectic. "Didn't you see the papers yesterday? Those foolish busybodies, Mother Nature's Avengers, went public! Everyone is on our tail! It's a war zone around this place! Wherever that blasted carcass of a motorcycle is, Einfinger, someone's going to identify it! So you get to that motorcycle before every last scrap of useful *materiel* is washed away in spring rainstorms!"

"But—" said Einfinger, to the sound of a slammed-down receiver.

When Thekla Mustard got home, she phoned an all-points bulletin to her fellow Tattletales. "Get on your bikes, get a ride, I don't care how, get over here," she told them. "On the double. People, we have a situation developing that the Tattletales need to know about."

Thekla's word was law. Carly, Nina, Anna Maria, Fawn, and Sharday met on Thekla's front porch within minutes.

"Girls," declaimed Thekla, "my little friends, my subjects, my abjects, my minions: I have something to say to you."

Right about here was when Lois would usually say something withering. But Lois had been fired from the Tattletales, and there was no withering remark to be heard. None of the other girls could think of anything to say to deflate Thekla. So she just kept inflating.

"I have decided that we must let bygones be bygones. I am granting full diplomatic immunity to Lois Kennedy the Third. The poor girl has suffered enough. Back to the fold she must come."

The Tattletales looked at each other. Charity was not what Thekla was best known for. Thekla peered through her glasses at them. "What? You think I'm not capable of reversals of mood? You think I can't grow and change and become even more grand than I was? I am not just Thekla Mustard to you. I am not just your Empress. I think I am going to call myself La Mustard. The one and only Thek La Mustard. Able to spill kindness and goodwill toward all, even those who don't deserve it one bit. Like Lois."

"Thekla," said Sharday, "what you yammering on about?"

"I don't yammer," said Thekla. "I pontificate. There's a difference."

"Well, La Mustard, explain some more, 'cause we don't get it."

"Lois, currently a member of that upstart rival group called the Three Rotten Eggs, is the adoptive stepparent of a newly hatched chick. A chick, I might add, that is cute and sweet and all that stuff. Also capable of burning down the town if it gets loose."

The other girls leaned forward. What was *this* new wrinkle?

"My dear subjects, those chicks have a very roasty-toasty sort of bad breath. And I can't allow Lois to prance about town babysitting a—what did they call it?—a Flame-burper. She docsn't have the stature. She'd be too snobby to bear. She must be brought back into the fold. Whether she wants to or not." That sounded more like the real Thekla. "We Tattletales must take some control of this situation. Are you with me?"

Nobody nodded.

"Thekla," said Fawn in her small voice, "why do you have to rule the world?"

"Why does any mad scientist or evil dictator want to rule the world?" said Thekla crossly. "Because it's there to be ruled, that's why. If I don't do it, somebody else will do it. Like, maybe, that Thud. And who would you trust more at the helm of the world? Thud Tweed or La Mustard?"

No one offered an opinion.

"See?" said Thekla, deciding to interpret the silence as cowed submission. "Now: a committee to go persuade Lois to rejoin. Who wants to be on it?"

"When do we get to see the Flameburpers?" asked Anna Maria.

"Not a *word* to a *soul* about those Flameburpers!" snapped Thekla.

Sammy Grubb was having much the same idea. He didn't convene a meeting of the Copycats, though. He just got on the phone when he got home and called Salim Bannerjee's house. "Hi, Salim," said Sammy.

"Hello, Sammy," said Salim in a voice more stiff and formal than usual.

"Hey, you know what, Salim?" said Sammy. "I'm sorry I was so angry at you about the egg hunt. That was small of me. It was just an egg hunt."

"I see," said Salim, in a voice that didn't sound very convinced.

"I wish you would come back to the Copycats," said Sammy Grubb.

"I like my new friends," said Salim.

"But isn't Thud a bit rough? He threatened me and Thekla," said Sammy Grubb.

"He's the Boss of the Three Rotten Eggs, and I am a Rotten Egg now," said Salim.

"I'd like you to quit the Rotten Eggs and come back to being a Copycat," said Sammy Grubb. "I'll make you my Deputy Chief. When I'm sick or out of town, you can be in charge."

"Thank you," said Salim. "I'll consider the offer. But I have no answer for you at the moment."

"Okay," said Sammy Grubb easily. "Take your time. Just one more thing, Salim. Do those chicks really breathe flames?"

"They did at first," said Salim, "but now that there are three of them, they are learning to keep their fiery opinions to themselves. I think it's like babies learning not to bite by having someone bite them back. The chicks are a bit flamboyant, if that's the word. Or do I mean inflammatory? But I'm not worried that they are going to burn down the town or anything."

"Good," said Sammy. "Because don't forget there are gasoline tanks in the front of Clumpett's General Store. If a chick happened to burp a little flame near the tanks—well, it'd be raining fire down on the town for weeks."

"Thank you for the advice," said Salim. "I appreciate your calling. I'll get back to you. But Sammy? In the meantime? Please keep the news of the Flameburpers to yourself. We don't want them hounded by the press in their formative early days."

Salim sounded sad, as if he thought that Sammy Grubb had been calling just to get a Flameburper chick under the thumb of the Copycats. Well, Sammy admitted to himself as he hung up the phone, if Salim felt that way, he'd be partly right. No wonder Salim hadn't accepted his offer yet.

Lois Kennedy the Third was walking her dog, Reebok, on the road near Old Man Fingerpie's farm when Flossie Fingerpie came outside with some slops for the pig. "Hello there, Lois!" called Flossie. "How's our Doozy doing for you?"

"The eggs are hatched, Mrs. Fingerpie," Lois answered. "Doozy's being a great stepmother."

"Not surprised. Doozy's got a head on her shoulders," said Flossie. "It's a little head, as heads go, but it's still there. Unlike Minerva's, since we stewed her for supper on Sunday. I'll tell Old Man. If he can focus long enough to take it all in, he'll be pleased as a pickle in a puddle of brine. How long you think you'll need Doozy's services?"

"Oh, the book says a couple of weeks anyway," said Lois.

"Well, take good care of her," said Flossie, and went into the barn.

Anna Maria and Fawn came huffing up the hill on their bikes. "Hi, Lois," they wheezed, and dropped their bikes to the ground. Reebok bounded around them, barking with pleasure.

"Oh, it's you," said Lois. "I suppose Thekla sent you?"

"Thekla's not in charge of *everything* we do," said Anna Maria.

"Yes, she did send us," said Fawn, who didn't think she was good at lying and so rarely bothered to try. "We're here to invite you back to the Tattletales. Thekla said she's sorry."

Thekla had never said any such thing, so Fawn was perhaps better at lying than she thought.

"Thekla said she's sorry?" said Lois. "Really?"

"She wants you to come back and bring that chick she calls a Flameburper with you," said Anna Maria. "She thinks it should be a Tattletale chick, raised under the rubrics and traditions of Tattletale society."

"Oh, she does?" said Lois. "Well, what if I think otherwise?"

"I suppose she'd listen to your opinions. Or pretend to."

Lois paused a minute to think. She didn't want to abandon Salim. But Thud? Thud still seemed sort of menacing. And she had to think of her precious little Beatrice. If Thud's chick, Amos, became a bully like Thud, baby Beatrice might be affected. Peer pressure and all that. Maybe it would be better for the chicks to be raised separately.

"Okay," she said. "I don't really want to come, but I have to think of Beatrice. For me to rejoin the Tattletales would be in her best interest. As soon as Beatrice is old enough to leave her stepmother and enter the wide world of

Tattletaledom, I'll come back. You can take this message to your Empress. But also tell her to keep her great big fat flapping mouth shut about the Flameburpers. It's classified information. Got it?

"Got it," said Anna Maria. "You won't be sorry, Lois."

"Oh, you probably will," said Fawn, "but I'm glad you're coming back anyway. We've missed you, Lois."

Lois was surprised how happy she felt to hear that she'd been missed. She skipped all the way home.

18. Trooper Crawdad Looks In

Einfinger was getting desperate. He didn't dare call the Vermont State Trooper headquarters again and speak to that Trooper Hiram Crawdad. Thanks to the press leak, Trooper Crawdad might be putting the story together. He might be getting a security force in place around the motorcycle.

And it didn't help any to hear that there were three giant chicks in Strafford. Einfinger spent hours tracking them down to a barn in the Upper Village, only to find that they were not miraculous survivors of a lightning strike but three giant, nine-foot velour-and-papier-mâché chickies being built for the annual Bread and Puppets outdoor summer festival they used to have in Glover.

Trooper Hiram Crawdad smiled as he pulled up in front of Clumpett's General Store in the middle of Hamlet, Vermont. It was an early-release day and spring was here. There was a steady stream of kids arriving from the direction of the grade school. They all wanted their penny candy, their jawbreakers, their Tootsie Rolls. The sight made him feel like buying an ice cream sandwich. But when he went inside, he saw that the kids weren't clustered around the candy counter or sneaking peeks at the comic books. One by one they were asking permission to go behind the meat counter and head out the back door. Bucky Clumpett was saying, one by one, "Ay-yup. As you like. Ay-yup. Be my guest. Ay-yup. After you. Ay-yup."

Trooper Crawdad fixed himself a cup of coffee and paid Olympia Clumpett for it. She tossed the coins in the jar for the fire engine fund. "We're seeing a lot of you these days," she said.

"Well, I called back the Einfinger number and got a recording saying, 'All lines connecting to Geneworks, Inc., are down for repair. Goodbye.' So that *does* connect Professor Einfinger with the *Boston Globe* story. Thought I'd come tell you in case he shows up poking around."

"What if he does? It's a free country," said Olympia. "You saying he's trouble?"

"As far as I know, he's uprighter than a telephone pole. And altering genes may be ethically icky, but I don't know that it's illegal. No, I'm only saying it's suspicious. He appears to have lied to us. And he's a slick and somewhat nasty character. That's all. What's the big attraction in the back, by the way?"

Being an imaginative woman, Olympia Clumpett had already begun to see a possibility that neither Bucky nor Trooper Crawdad seemed to have arrived at yet. Could it be that some of those eggs had survived and hatched out those three chicks back there? While she struggled not to lie

121

about them, she also tried not to give vent to her suspicions, for after all, she had no proof. "Just some children doing a school project," she said.

"Is that so?" said Trooper Crawdad. "What's the project?"

"Well . . . it's raising farm animals," said Olympia Clumpett guardedly.

"Big animals or small animals?"

"Well, small so far. But they'll get bigger as they grow."

"I see," said Hiram. "Sounds the usual way."

"Very usual," said Olympia. "Rather boring, really, but you know kids."

"Are these animals—oh, say, cows?"

"Well," said Olympia Clumpett, as if trying to remember, "I don't think so."

"Might they be pigs?"

"They might be, but if so, very unusual pigs."

"Could you go so far as to call them ponies?"

"You could, but they probably wouldn't come if you did."

"I see," said Trooper Crawdad. The more he asked, the more intrusive he felt. "Are they anything like sheep?"

"They're a little like sheep," said Olympia, but then she felt bad that she was lying to an officer of the law. "Very little like sheep," she admitted.

"Farm animals, you say," said Trooper Crawdad, stroking his chin.

"Oh, they're little baby chicks, if you must know," said Olympia. "No law on earth says a chicken can't hatch some chicks of a fine spring afternoon, officer!"

"Indeed not," said Trooper Crawdad. "Mind if I see them?"

"I don't suppose I could stop you. Bucky," she called, "our friend from the state police is back."

"Howdy," said Bucky. "I'll mind the till, Limpy, if you want to take our visitor to have a gander at the little chicks."

Trooper Crawdad and Olympia Clumpett made their way past the cuts of meat out to the backyard. There the students of Miss Earth's class were sitting silently on the ground, holding their sides, trying to keep from roaring with laughter, as the three cutest little chicks you ever did see roamed the yard behind a rather exhausted-looking hen. The chicks looked as if they were playing Simon Says. If Thud got up and waggled his butt, the chicks all waggled their butts. When Lois did a somersault, the chicks followed suit. Salim did an impromptu dance in honor of the coming of spring, complete with sinuous motions of his arms, and the chicks imitated him as best they could, given that they had no arms. They were very impressionable and also very talented.

The students were laughing so hard that they never noticed Trooper Crawdad hovering behind them.

"They're like little Olympic gymnast chicks!" said Trooper Crawdad. The kids all turned and looked. Thud, Lois, and Salim turned pale. "How do you tell them apart?"

"That one is mine," said Thud, pointing to the red-yarn chick. With someone new to impress, Amos began running at the other chicks, crashing into them. He pushed them over and tried to stand on them.

Beatrice escaped and ran after Doozy to hide in the shadow of her rump. She bumped into it. When Doozy turned around, Beatrice just smiled in a saintly fashion and stood still as if she wasn't doing much of anything so what was Doozy staring at?

Seymour had a harder time escaping from Amos. Salim had to keep swooping in and rescuing him.

"I suppose that this good hen is the mother of these chicks?" asked Trooper Crawdad.

"You could reach that conclusion," said Olympia Clumpett cautiously. "Look how they follow her everywhere."

"Well, kids?" pressed Trooper Crawdad. "Did this hen lay these eggs? For the record, I should know the truth."

None of the children spoke except Thud. "Sure she did," he said, looking Trooper Crawdad in the eye. "Laid 'em, hatched 'em—the works."

"That's all I needed to know," said Trooper Crawdad. "I conclude then that this motorcycle was the one driven by one of Mother Nature's Avengers, and it carried Einfinger's experimental eggs. But they all got crushed, and these chicks are no relation at all. And since Einfinger disavows any further interest in the matter, I'm under no special obligation to continue in my efforts to inform him of my discovery."

"I did see the eggs, all crushed and ruined," said Olympia Clumpett, and she was telling the truth as far as she knew it. But she was relieved to know that these weren't genetically mutated chicks. Otherwise, the Geneworks scientists might be on the lookout for them.

"You going to be filing any reports on springtime farm animals, officer?" asked Olympia as she led him back into the store.

"Don't see why I should," said Trooper Crawdad. "Especially with the word of that big lad. Vermonters tell the truth. So I believe him."

Olympia didn't think that Thud was a native-born Vermonter, but she kept her mouth shut. Anyway, none of the other children had contradicted his statement. And they *were* all good Vermont kids, every last one of them. Even Salim from Bombay, India, qualified as a good Vermont kid by now.

19. The Truth Comes Out

On her way home from work, Mrs. Bannerjee stopped at Clumpett's to pick up some eggs for dinner. She noticed the children gathered outside the back door, and she asked permission to go past the meat coolers and see what the fuss was. As luck would have it, Miss Earth had also run in to buy a bottle of extra-strength aspirin. She joined Mrs. Bannerjee at the back door of the shop.

"I see Doozy Dorking is being a good foster mother," said Miss Earth.

"Hello, Salim," said Mrs. Bannerjee. "You have a lovely little chick in your hands. It it yours?"

"Yes, Mama. His name is Seymour."

"That must be a very American name," said Mrs. Bannerjee approvingly. She wanted her son to feel at home in this great land of his, and hers, and everyone else's. "I never heard of it before. Seymour. Sounds dignified."

Salim wished his mother would go home. He knew his former Copycat friends were still angry that she had given

126

the Tattletales all the Copycats' eggs. But Mrs. Bannerjee had picked up that something was wrong with Salim at school, and she wanted it to get better. She lingered, cooing at the chicks, laughing at Beatrice's antics, protesting when Amos played a rather nasty version of chicken with the other chicks. "Oh, the little sweeties!" she said. "Whose is that funny little chick who keeps jumping up and down like a gymnast with tics in its legs?"

"That's mine," said Lois, "and her name is Beatrice. And the aggressive one is called Amos, and he belongs to Thud. This is Thud, Mrs. Bannerjee."

Mrs. Bannerjee looked around. "Oh, Thud!" she said. "I remember you from the egg hunt. You're the one who told me to share Salim's eggs with the girls."

Thud turned a little red. "You're mixing me up with somebody else," he mumbled.

"Oh, heavens, never would I do that!" said Mrs. Bannerjee jovially. "You are far bigger and stouter than the other children. I couldn't confuse you with anyone else. It is nice to see you again, Master Thud."

The Copycats turned, one after another: Forest Eugene, Stan, Hector, Moshe, Mike, and Sammy Grubb. Salim turned, too. They looked at Thud Tweed with glowering expressions. "*You* told Salim's parents to hand over the eggs to the girls?" asked Sammy Grubb in a very brittle voice.

"They don't understand English," said Thud. "They didn't understand what I was saying."

"Of course I understand English!" cried Mrs. Bannerjee. "English was one of my mother tongues in India."

"Mom," said Salim, "I think you had better go home and take me with you."

"Say good night to your chick," said Mrs. Bannerjee.

"Goodbye, Seymour," said Salim dourly. "Don't let Amos cheat and lie to you the way some humans do. Oh, and by the way, Thud, I quit the Rotten Eggs. Effective immediately. I'm going to go back and be a Copycat. I'd rather copy rightness than cunning."

Sammy nodded solemnly, approving the readmission to the club. Then Salim left, dragging his mother after him.

But Miss Earth stood stock still and looked down at her remaining students. "Do I understand, Thaddeus Nero Tweed," she said, "that you lied to Salim's mother in order to help the girls cheat?"

Thud didn't answer.

"And am I to believe that you girls racked up your hoard of eggs by siphoning off the supply of the boys' eggs?" said Miss Earth to the Tattletales.

"I didn't," said Pearl, reminding everyone that she wasn't a Tattletale.

"There's no rule against it," said Thekla Mustard to her teacher. She was blushing with shame, but she couldn't lie. "No one said that the eggs had to be *found* to be counted. Only that they had to be *handed in* to be counted. Anyway, I didn't know that he suggested it." Thekla pointed to Thud. "So it's his fault."

"Lois was the one who told Salim to ask his parents to guard the eggs," said Thud. "It's her fault."

"Sammy was the one who wouldn't let Salim hunt for eggs in his very first egg hunt!" said Lois. "It's his fault."

"Thekla was the one who suggested that we make it a competition between the Copycats and the Tattletales!" said Sammy. "It's her fault."

"I don't like this at all," said Miss Earth. "It's a good thing I have some extra-strength aspirin. I feel a headache like a thunderstorm coming on." She could barely speak. She turned on her heel and left without saying goodbye.

"Thanks a lot," said Lois. "You've really helped our class a lot, Boss Thud."

"What do I care about *our class?*" said Thud. "I care about the Three Rotten Eggs. And not much else."

Lois petted Beatrice for a moment without speaking. Then she stood up. "I may not like Thekla Mustard, but at least she doesn't *lie,*" said Lois. "When faced with Miss Earth's question, she told the truth and braved the consequences."

Thekla didn't look up and preen, for once.

"I'm going back to the Tattletales," concluded Lois. "So long, Boss. I quit the Rotten Eggs, as of here and now."

cheating
lying
self-esteem

20. The Anger of Miss Earth

On Friday morning, Trooper Hiram Crawdad said to his superior, "I don't think those little chicks I saw could be genetic mutants. They were so cute. Besides, I met their mother, a decent dignified Vermont hen with impeccable manners."

"All mutants aren't monsters," said his supervisor. "I think you should keep an eye on 'em, Trooper. Just in case. Those kids could have been lying to you."

"Lying to a *Vermont state trooper?*" said Trooper Crawdad.

"Go back up there and get some corroboration from a grownup, if you can."

"A motorcycle driver?" groused a farmer at the hay-and-feed store. "Nobody in Chumptown Falls rides a motorcycle, for the plain truth that you can't get four-wheel drive out of a two-wheel vehicle. Shoot, once mud season arrives, I can hardly get four-wheel drive on Bossy, my four-legged cow. But I hear there's a teacher lady in one of the local grade schools who rides a motorcycle. Maybe she's a member of some secret Vermont higher education motorcycle gang. Maybe she'd know."

The farmer laughed to show it was a joke. But Einfinger had to follow up every lead, however slim. Since lightning strikes were turning out to be a dime a dozen in these hills, maybe he should find that teacher lady and put his questions about motorcycle sightings to her.

That same Friday, when the students arrived at the Josiah Fawcett Elementary School, they were greeted with an unfamiliar chilliness. Miss Earth stood at her desk with her arms folded. Her usual bright expression was gone, replaced by a look of sad determination. "Take your seats, children," she said as they came galloping into the room.

She took the roll.

"Salim Bannerjee?"

"Here, Miss Earth."

"Nina Bueno?"

"Present, Miss Earth."

"All the rest of you?" said Miss Earth tiredly, flipping the attendance book onto the desk with a sudden impatience.

"Here, Miss Earth."

"Anyone not here, raise your hand."

No one raised a hand.

"Good," said Miss Earth. "My sixteen students, from Salim Bannerjee to Hector Yellow, are all present. I'm glad. You need to hear something. While we're waiting, I want you to take out some paper. Here are some key words." She scribbled some things on the board. *Cheating. Lying. Self-Esteem.* "This morning I want you to write me a few thoughts on one or more of these topics."

Pearl Hotchkiss raised her hand to ask a question.

"No questions," said Miss Earth. She sat down in her wooden chair and turned her back to the students. Was she taking a little white handkerchief out of her pocketbook and dabbing at the corners of her eyes?

The students struggled. Ordinarily, Miss Earth gave terrific writing assignments. This one was tough. Most of the students wrote the usual stuff about how being good was better than being bad, since being bad was worse than being good.

It was hard to be inventive with such a topic.

The door opened. In walked Principal Buttle, followed by Trooper Hiram Crawdad. The class stood as one—even Thud, who had never stood to greet an adult in his life.

"Good *morning,* Principal Buttle," they singsonged, as they had been taught to do since kindergarten. Then they sat down again.

"I believe there's some doubt as to how good it is," said Principal Hetty Buttle. She looked down her long, elegant nose at Miss Earth's students. "Class, I would like to introduce you to Trooper Hiram Crawdad of the Vermont State Police. He is here on some official business. I have some of my own."

Trooper Hiram Crawdad had not been in a grade school since he had graduated from a one-room schoolhouse in the Northeast Kingdom. He was a little nervous. He twisted his hat in his hands and cleared his throat. "There's been a lot in the news lately about an abandoned motorcycle and its cargo of stolen eggs," he said. "I think I've found the motorcycle, and I found the briefcase the eggs came in. Now, just to be doubly sure I have all the facts, I have come to ask you a question, and I want an honest answer."

Thud leaped to his feet. "All right. I confess. I stole the eggs we hatched from an Easter display over in Hanover. There was a big fat lady with asthma, and she kept choking into her apron, and I thought she might be allergic to chicken fuzz, so when the ambulance came I–"

But Salim and Lois looked across the room at each other and stood up at the same time.

"Trooper," said Salim, "I can tell you what I know."

"And I can vouch for it," said Lois. "Those eggs aren't from Hanover."

"But we want no harm to come to our chicks," said Salim.

Thud slumped back in his seat and put his head on his desk.

"I'm as fond of chicks as the next one," said Trooper Crawdad, "but I make no promises. I can't."

Salim and Lois told the story of how the Three Rotten Eggs had come upon the three unbroken stolen eggs and removed them from the wreckage of the motorcycle. Principal Buttle looked like stone. Miss Earth put her hand to her mouth.

"It's my duty to call in this report to my sergeant," said Trooper Crawdad. He whipped out a cell phone and stepped out of the room to place the call. "Don't anyone leave the premises."

"As if," said Miss Earth darkly.

"Meanwhile," said Principal Buttle, "I have something else to say. I've been in touch with the town selectmen. We have decided to disqualify Miss Earth's class from the egg-hunting competition. We are revoking your status as winners and naming Mr. Pilsky's second-grade class the winners instead."

"But that's no fair!" said Thekla Mustard. "We won fair and square!"

"You won square," said Principal Buttle, "in that together, boys and girls, you did find more eggs than any other class. But you didn't win fair. I understand from Miss Earth that there was lying and cheating and deceit going on among your class members. And there is no adult in the town who can sanction that."

"But," sputtered Thekla Mustard, "I've already collected sixteen dollars apiece from my pledges!"

"Give it back," said the principal. "We'll have to raise money another way. We don't run a fundraising event so that our students can learn to cheat and lie."

The children felt horrible. They all looked at Thud. It was all his fault! None of them had ever cheated or lied in their lives. Well, not seriously.

"And I'll have the amendment printed in next week's *Hamlet Holler*," said Principal Buttle. "So everyone in town can see what you students are up to."

"No!" whined the students.

"And I'm going to go have a chat with Old Man Fingerpie," said Trooper Crawdad, stepping back in the room, "and find out when those chicks can be safely taken from Doozy Dorking. Because as soon as they can be separated, I have to take those chicks into protective custody. They are stolen goods. Let the courts decide what happens to them."

"Noooooooo!" wailed the students, even Thud.

"Yes, indeedy," said Trooper Crawdad. "My supervising

officer has spoken. Now, if I were you, I would keep this little larceny of yours from general knowledge around town. Word gets out, we'll have Geneworks goons crawling around here trying to kidnap these chicks in an instant." He glared at them. "Frankly, I'm surprised at you good Vermont children." He left the room.

"Children," said Miss Earth, "the ethics of genetic experimentation are difficult to sort out. We have never talked about this. I can see that you might have an instinct to protect the feeble and defenseless chicks, whether genetically freakish or not. Frankly, I would feel the same, I suppose. But to know that you have all lied to an officer of the law—well, words fail me."

"Miss Earth." Thekla Mustard was standing up. "I want to point out that nothing so bad ever happened in this classroom until a certain Master Thaddeus Tweed transferred to our school. Technically speaking, his words were the lying ones. We other children were merely silent. Call us shy. Do you think it's possible to have him removed to another school? I believe he is infecting us with his wicked ways."

"Thekla Mustard," said Miss Earth, "I never thought I'd say such a thing to any pupil of mine, but I can't control myself. Sit down. If you can't take responsibility for your own actions, Thekla, you're not fit to govern anyone else. If I were a Tattletale, I'd boot you out of office so fast, your head would spin. Because sometimes, Thekla, you can be quite a little stinker."

21. The Big Idea

"Oh, sure," said a gas station attendant in Puster Center. "You're looking for Miss Earth. She teaches at the Josiah Fawcett School over to Hamlet. Stops here for a fill-up anytime she's out this way. She drives a Kawasaki 8000 Silver Eagle. Prettiest little thing you ever did see."

The teacher or the motorcycle? wondered Einfinger, and went to check the map to see where Hamlet was.

"I can give you a shortcut," said the attendant. "It's an unmarked old logging trail, runs up over Hardscrabble Hill and down into Route 12. Get you there in a flash, if you're in a hurry." He marked the route with a pencil. "Just turn left beyond the maple sugar collective. You can't miss it."

Miss Earth was too angry with her students to do any teaching. She walked around the classroom in a snit, folding her arms, huffing. Her children slunk down over their social studies textbooks, reading hour after hour.

At lunchtime, Miss Earth sat with her celery tonic and

her diet yogurt and a couple of jelly doughnuts. She couldn't eat a bite. She was too upset. Mr. Pilsky, the second-grade teacher, said, "I'll have a doughnut if you don't want it."

"Go ahead. You deserve it. Your class won the competition," she said.

"The second graders are over the moon about it," he admitted. "It's hard to explain to them about why they won now, seven days later, rather than on the day of the hunt. I hated having to tell them the reason."

"I always thought good teaching made all the difference," said Miss Earth. "Or at least some of the difference. But maybe Thekla Mustard is right. Maybe Thud Tweed is a rotten kid. Maybe he is spoiling my class. I hate to give up on him. But I don't like these developments. I don't want my nice kids to become thugs and hooligans, liars and cheaters. Maybe I should just quit teaching if I can't do my job right."

On the playground at lunchtime Miss Earth's students did not break up into factions for once. Together Pearl Hotchkiss, the Tattletales, the Copycats, and Thud Tweed, the last remaining member of the Three Rotten Eggs, stood in a clump in the middle of the yard.

Pearl Hotchkiss was the first to break the silence. "Frankly," she said, "I think Miss Earth is right. The Copycats' and Tattletales' competition has gone—how shall I say it?—*stale*. The Rotten Eggs was a little relief, but it has gotten out of hand, too. Either we are together as Miss Earth's students or we don't deserve to have her as our teacher."

"Maybe we *don't* deserve it," said Fawn Petros in a small voice.

"We can be sorry," said Sammy Grubb. "Can't we? It's not like we've killed anyone. Can't we move on?"

"But what can we do to prove to Miss Earth how sorry we are?" asked Lois Kennedy the Third.

"We could choreograph a dance celebrating her winning ways," said Sharday Wren, who took ballet, tap, and modern.

"We could honor her by awarding an annual Miss Earth prize to the student who had the highest average in the class," said Moshe Cohn, who had the highest average in the class.

"I could make the statuette out of plaster of Paris," said Hector Yellow, who liked to be artistic. "Instead of the Emmy or the Grammy, it could be called the Earthie."

Thekla Mustard said, "If you're all done exercising your lungs and tongues, I'll remind you that the real problem is that we have lost the chance to raise funds for the fire engine. What if we took it upon ourselves to raise money in some other fashion, and donate it to the fund drive? It could be seen as a public rehabilitation. But we wouldn't have to actually apologize." Thekla hated to apologize.

"But we were set to raise a lot of money," said Carly Garfunkel. "We'd have to raise about the same amount as we'd promised the fund. How could we do that?"

"We could put on a show!" said Sharday Wren. "I could do a little dance. It would go like this." She began to dance like a chick, which made the other kids laugh.

"That's ridiculous," said Thekla Mustard. "Who would come to pay to see us in a show? Only our parents. And everyone is angry with us. No, a show is a good idea, but it can't star us."

"I know," said Lois Kennedy the Third. "Let's get our old friend Meg Snoople on the phone again. Maybe she can fly her helicopter in and do another broadcast from Hamlet on her breakfast show."

"That wouldn't raise money," said Salim. "In India you have to have a television license, but in America TV is free."

"Doesn't Miss Earth love Petunia Whiner's music? We could get Petunia Whiner to come give a benefit concert," said Thud Tweed.

"How could we do that?" asked Mike Saint Michael.

"Easy," said Thud. "Petunia Whiner is my mother."

"Oh, cut it out," said Nina Bueno.

"It's true. She is," said Thud.

"You're not only a rotten egg, you're a rotten liar," said Carly. "Nobody could believe *that*."

"Just believe me, okay?"

"You *are* a liar," said Thekla. "We've all seen it."

Thud looked around. Sammy Grubb nodded. So did Salim and Lois, the other former Rotten Eggs, looking sad.

"All right," said Thud. "After school, everybody meet at my car. We'll go see for ourselves."

"Why should we bother?" cried Pearl. "Everything connected with you is trouble."

"I'm asking you to believe me," said Thud. "Here, you want me to say the magic word? *Please*. There."

He said it as if it were a foul word.

"Please," he repeated in a more normal voice. Not as a bullying command but—almost—as a request. "Please."

"Can you fit fifteen extra kids in your car?" asked Sammy Grubb.

"I'll call home and have them send the stretch limo," said Thud. "We'll stretch it."

Miss Earth piled on the weekend homework as if she thought they were about to break for three weeks. Nobody complained. They were all waiting to see how Thud would get out of his biggest lie yet.

When school let out, Sammy Grubb explained to the bus driver that none of Miss Earth's students were taking the school bus. Sammy was bus monitor, so the driver shrugged and pulled away. As soon as it was gone, the kids piled into the glamorous black vehicle and breathed in the royal smell of well-oiled leather and pine-scented deodorizer.

Thud Tweed slipped a CD into the car's audio system. It was the greatest hits of Petunia Whiner, Volume III. It included some of Miss Earth's favorites: "Stick with Your Man," "The Broken Banjo Blues," and, of course, the current hit, already a country-western classic, "Baby Needs Burping."

"That doesn't mean anything," said Thekla. "Anybody could buy a Petunia Whiner CD on Amazon dot com."

"Just wait," said Thud.

The limo drove west out of Hamlet. The kids frankly felt a little scared. What if Thud really was a maniac and was going to lock them in his house? Maybe they should have told someone where they were going.

Smoothly the limo turned west off Squished Toad Road, passing between brick pillars topped with granite spheres the size of beach balls. The driveway was a mile long. Then out of the woods the driveway wound around the swell of an apron of emerald lawn without a single dandelion on it. The old Munning house was huge and cold, built of gray granite.

The kids tumbled out of the car and followed Thud up the stone steps. He opened the door and led them into the front hall. The atrium went up three flights, and a gloomy light filtered down through a colored stained-glass skylight. "Tiffany glass," said Thud.

"Who's that, some backup singer of your mom's?" asked Sharday Wren.

"I'm home, Mom!" bellowed Thud.

They heard the sound of a door opening upstairs, and a voice with an English accent said, "Did I hear the bleat of my offspring?"

"I said I'm home," yelled Thud. "I brought some kids from school."

For a moment or two there was silence. Then the voice said drily, "Friends? Or prisoners?"

Thud wasn't sure how to answer this, so he didn't.

Mrs. Tweed appeared at the top of the marble staircase. As usual, she was dressed sensibly, in a dignified wool skirt and a white blouse. A pink angora sweater clung to her shoulders, offering protection against the chill. Her hair was cut short and managed with mousse. Her earrings were pearls. Her necklace was pearls. Her teeth were pearls. "Children," said Mrs. Tweed, as if she'd never seen any before, and Thud didn't count, Thud being more like a buffalo than a child. She approached them.

"Mom," said Thud, "I hate to do this to you, but these kids want to know if you're Petunia Whiner."

"My name is Mildred Tweed," said Thud's mother.

"Right," said Thud. "And your stage name?"

"Don't do this to me, Thaddeus."

141

"I can't help it," he said. "It's important, Mom."

"Why?" she asked.

"Because," he answered. "Mom, I'm used to lying, but for once I'm trying to tell the truth. And for once you're not on tour when I need your help."

She got a funny look on her face. It was almost tender. She sighed. "Maybe Miss Earth was right. Maybe I need to take a larger role in your educational career." She sat down demurely on a chair with gilt legs and a scalloped back. She crossed her ankles and put her hands genteelly in her lap, as if she had just been elected the first woman pope. "Maybe one way to say it is this: I should pay more attention to what I sing. My own baby, who never talks to me, has asked for help. My baby needs burping.

"Yes, children, it is true. I am Petunia Whiner."

Thekla Mustard pushed forward. She leaned down and studied Mrs. Tweed. "I don't believe it," she said at last. "You're as big a liar as your son. That's where he gets it."

"I confess. I am a liar. I have been hiding my identity from you locals. But I am, indeed, Petunia Whiner."

"You don't have big hair," said Stan Tomaski.

"Wigs," said Mrs. Tweed. "Big heavy hairpieces."

"You have an English accent," said Anna Maria Mastrangelo.

"I grew up in Mayfair, a neighborhood in London," said Mrs. Tweed.

"You act as quiet and shy as a part-time librarian!" said Forest Eugene Mopp.

"I resent that," said Mrs. Tweed. "Who says that part-time librarians have to be shy? I *was* a part-time librarian once, and that's how my singing career got started. To raise funds for the library budget I did a comedy number as an American country-western singer. I was a smash hit."

"You are a *very capable* liar," said Thekla Mustard. "Thud, I see where you get it. Come on, kids," she said in disgust, "let's get outta here."

"Mom," said Thud, "please?"

Mrs. Tweed stood. She pressed her hands on the front of her dress, smoothing the wrinkles from her waistline downward. She cleared her throat mildly, as if about to summon the waitress for another cup of tea. Then she threw back her head and out it came. Sweet thunder. Liquid dynamite. Vintage Petunia.

> *"Ya got a little baby and ya gotta treat it right!*
> *Ya gotta rock the cradle so your baby sleeps tight!*
> *Baby needs a diaper change, Baby has a poo.*
> *If Baby wakes and burps a lot, whatcha gonna do?"*

"You've made your point!" shrieked Thekla, but no one could hear her, because the other kids too were shrieking, like insane fans at a rock concert. Everyone joined in:

> *"Just cuddle cuddle cuddle till the cows come home!"*

Mrs. Tweed struck a pose with her hands on her hips and her shoulders thrown back and her head aimed up at the Tiffany glass skylight three stories overhead. The effect was stunning.

22. The Apology Committee

Professor Wolfgang Einfinger finally pulled up in front of Clumpett's General Store in Hamlet, Vermont. The unmarked logging trail over Hardscrabble Hill had been little better than an endless track of mud. His car had gotten stuck four or five times, and having had to dig it out, Einfinger was filthy. The exercise had cost him several hours. However, the middle-aged cashier didn't seem to mind giving directions to a mud-caked stranger. She pointed out the way to the Josiah Fawcett Elementary School. But by the time Einfinger got there, the doors were locked for the weekend.

He went back to the store and asked for a recommendation for a bed-and-breakfast for the evening. Widow Wendell's Lovey Inn had a room available. He checked in and had a shower to clean up and make himself respectable. Then he tried to get Miss Earth on the phone. An older woman answered the phone and said that her daughter was in the bath, preparing to go out on a date with the mayor. Oh, well, tomorrow morning, then. Einfinger had waited this long. He could wait a few hours more.

After the children and Mrs. Tweed had discussed the details of mounting a concert, the chauffeur drove the children back to town. Thud went with them.

"So just tell us one thing, Thud," said Sammy Grubb. "Was your dad really a magazine publisher in Milan or a casino operator in Calcutta or in the Witness Protection Program, or what?"

"A little of everything, in a way," said Thud. "He was a Hollywood screenwriter. He wrote all those characters in his best-known film, *Lady and the Trampoline*. He died of internal injuries following a helicopter crash while he was flying to the film location."

"How long ago?" asked Salim Bannerjee.

Thud paused. "Never ago," he said. "I'm lying again. It's become a habit."

The children waited. Thud sighed. "I guess I have to tell the truth for once. Usually I go to boarding schools until I get kicked out of them. But my dad was jailed last month for tax fraud and grand larceny. That's lying and stealing. My mom thought I might need her company, since the news was all over the papers. And she couldn't take the shame of it, either. So she hid herself and me up here in deepest Vermont. On Sunday she's leaving to visit him in prison for the first time. That's why she has to do the concert Saturday night or not at all."

"So she's not dying of a terrible illness?" asked Thekla.

"She's dying of shame," said Thud. "She loves to perform, but she hasn't had the nerve since my dad was sent to prison."

No one knew what to say. Thud was a liar, and so was his mother. Apparently, his father was, too. But did that mean they would be liars forever? And that they couldn't change? It was spring, after all. Time for change.

The children had other questions. It was too sad to ask questions, though. They sat in silence until the chauffeur drove up to the green. Then they got out. Thud hung out with them, telling the chauffeur he'd find his own way home.

It was a beautiful late afternoon, the kind of day in spring when summer is hovering in the wings. In one garden some birds chattered about nothing much; in the garden next door some snowdrops bobbed their heads in agreement. You could almost smell the first hint of summer vacation in the air, though it was still several months away. It smelled strong and good.

The kids wandered to the backyard of Clumpett's General Store. Doozy Dorking was looking in need of a pick-me-up, a tonic made especially for hens. The chicks had perfected a game in which they lined up and faced Doozy and all kicked their little feet at the same time. Except Beatrice kept kicking the wrong foot, or maybe she was just doing that to be funny. She kept tripping Amos and making him fall on his face.

"Cluck," said Doozy. "Cluck cluck cluck."

Kick, went the chicks, kick kick kick.

"They're so coordinated," said Thud. "They have different personalities, but they all seem to have the same talent."

"Cluck," said Doozy, and did a little dip, as if about to lower herself into a fine dust bath. "Cluck cluck cluck."

Dip, went the chicks, in perfect time, waggling their little yellow butts in the air, dip dip dip.

"Hard to imagine what's going on in their little minds," said Lois.

Thud said, "Dancing chicks. Maybe they could be the warm-up act for Mom."

"Not likely," said Thekla. "With Geneworks bozos on the hunt for them? Now, kids, let's pay attention. We have work to do. I hate to pull rank, but as Empress of the Tattletales, I've had many years of experience in managing campaigns. I nominate myself to be on the committee that speaks with Miss Earth about our plan."

"As Chief of the Copycats, I should go, too," said Sammy Grubb.

"As the token holdout," said Pearl Hotchkiss, "I suppose I should go to represent the free thinkers among us. Namely, myself."

"As the last remaining Rotten Egg," said Thud, "what about me?"

Lois said, "How many people in favor of having Thud join the Apology Committee?"

Everyone raised a hand. The vote was unanimous, since Thud voted for himself.

"Hey, look," said Sammy Grubb. "The chicks are voting, too." And they were. Each chick had raised a little wing as far as it would go, which wasn't very. Only Doozy Dorking abstained from a vote. She had twisted her head to nibble some nits off her sloping shoulders.

Miss Earth was having her Friday-night bath, with extra bubbles, when she heard the phone ring. Her mother, Grandma Earth, was downstairs. She'd get it. Miss Earth leaned back in the tub and massaged her aching temples.

She'd never had such a teaching challenge as Thud Tweed. Maybe she should change professions. Should she take up a career as a professional skydiver? Or she could be a first lieutenant in the war against drugs. There was the McDonald's over in West Lebanon; they were always looking for counter help.

Then the doorbell rang. What a busy Friday evening! "Germy," said her mother, knocking at the bathroom door, "some of your kids here to see you."

"I'm not home," said Miss Earth crossly.

"Don't lie, Miss Earth," called Thud up the stairs. "We can hear you talking to your mother."

"That's a figure of speech, to say I'm not home," she yelled through her mounds of bubbles. But not wanting to give the wrong impression, she quickly toweled herself off and threw on a pair of jeans and a blouse. When she came downstairs, she saw her mother had served the kids tall glasses of milk and a plate of homemade cookies. "I'm usually not available for consultation at this hour," said Miss Earth. "What's up?"

Everyone knew Miss Earth admired Pearl Hotchkiss for not belonging to a club. So Pearl was the first one to speak. She sketched the children's hopes to raise money for the fire engine fund drive by selling tickets to a performance . . . by none other than noted country-western singer Petunia Whiner.

"Oh, please," said Miss Earth. "My head hurts. Petunia Whiner lives in Nashville or Hollywood or some penthouse on Fifth Avenue in Manhattan."

"Don't be so sure," said Pearl. "Petunia Whiner is an alias. Her real name is Mildred Tweed. She's Thud's mom.

She's willing to do a concert, but it has to be soon. Like tomorrow night. She's leaving Sunday evening to go see her husband, who's smashing rocks in the slammer. Out of love for her son, she's been persuaded to come out of retirement in a big way."

"Your father is in a federal penitentiary?" said Miss Earth. "Thud, we have to talk about telling the truth a little bit more than you're used to."

"It's true," chorused the children. "He is telling the truth."

"Well, wonders will never cease," said Miss Earth, thinking of her failed efforts to persuade Mrs. Tweed to take an interest in her son's school life. "My students have succeeded at a campaign I could not get off the ground. Well, good for you. But can we mount a benefit concert on such short notice?"

"Not you," said Pearl firmly. "*Us.* We'll do it. It's our job. We just want you to know our intentions and make sure that your calendar is clear tomorrow night."

"Mom?" said Miss Earth.

Grandma Earth, who had been hovering just out of sight in the kitchen, appeared instantly.

"We don't have plans tomorrow night, do we?"

"I've never much liked country-western music, preferring as I do acid rock, at eardrum-splitting decibel levels," said Grandma Earth. "But in a good cause, I could always come to a benefit concert and put cotton in my ears, I guess."

"All right," said Miss Earth. "If you arrange it, we'll be there. But what is this all about, really?"

"We want to let you know we're sorry," said Pearl.

"I'm sorry for giving Salim's parents the wrong idea about the eggs," said Thud.

"I'm sorry for instructing my Tattletales to take advantage of the Bannerjee parents," said Thekla.

"I'm sorry for giving Salim the cold shoulder afterward," said Sammy Grubb. "Boy, that was lousy of me."

"I'm not sorry for anything," said Pearl, "except in a general way, of course."

"Apologies accepted," said Miss Earth. "From all of you. Not so much because of the concert idea, though I admire your zeal. But because I like it better when you all work together. And even Thud is becoming a part of the class."

"Not really," said Thud. "But the Whiner is my mom. They can't move a step without my say-so." He rolled his eyes at Thekla, Sammy, and Pearl, but in a somewhat affectionate way. Miss Earth was not fooled for a moment. Thud was one of her students at last.

At seven A.M. on Saturday morning, the children sprang into action.

Sammy Grubb rode his bike over to the Vermont Museum of Interesting Things to Know and Tell. Mayor Grass lived in an apartment up above it. Mayor Grass was surprised to be awakened at that hour by a grade-school boy. But as a chairperson of the Board of Selectmen, Tim Grass didn't answer only to parents. "How can I help you, Sammy?" he asked groggily, leaning out his upstairs window.

Sammy explained the situation and asked for advice on where they could hold a concert to benefit the fire engine fund drive.

"After winter ice dams and water damage, the high

school auditorium walls are being repaired this weekend," said Mayor Grass. "I'm volunteering to do some of the painting today myself."

"How about the grade-school auditorium?"

"Frankly, I heard last night from Miss Earth that Principal Buttle has had it up to here with you kids," said Mayor Grass. "Why don't you ask Forest Eugene Mopp's mother? She's the minister of the Congregational/Unitarian church. Maybe she'll let you use their church hall. It's bigger than Saint Mary in the Tombstones."

"Gotcha. Can we count on your coming and putting down ten bucks for a ticket?"

"I'll be mighty tired, especially being woken at seven A.M. and working all day," said Mayor Grass, yawning.

"Miss Earth will be there," said Sammy Grubb slyly.

"Put me down for two tickets in the front row," said Mayor Grass, and slammed the window shut.

"So may we use the church hall?" asked Forest Eugene.

"Yes," said his mother, the Reverend Mrs. Mopp. "It's all for a good cause. But who's going to clean up after the concert? Ticket stubs and such?"

"We will," said Forest Eugene. "All of us."

"You bet you will," said the Reverend Mrs. Mopp. "And no gum chewing in church."

"Mom," said Forest Eugene, "nobody chews gum at a country-western concert."

"But how are you going to advertise it?" asked the Reverend Mrs. Mopp. "It's too late to get a notice in the *Hamlet Holler* or for me or Father Fogarty to announce it from our pulpits."

● ● ●

"Is that Ernie Latucci of WAAK, the Voice of Vermont?" asked Salim Bannerjee.

"Back atcha," said Ernie Lattuci, "on the air in twelve minutes, kid, and I still gotta have a potty moment, so lay it on me."

"A surprise benefit concert by country-western diva Petunia Whiner," said Salim Bannerjee. "The Hamlet Congregational/ Unitarian church on the green in Hamlet, Vermont. Tickets are available from Clumpett's General Store in Hamlet or, if there are any unsold ones left, at the door. Ten bucks a head, to benefit the fire engine fund drive."

"Cool," said Ernie. "When?"

"Tonight at eight."

"I'll announce it and I'll be there. Put me down for one ticket. May I broadcast the concert live on WAAK, the Voice of Vermont?"

"No," said Salim firmly. "Otherwise, everyone would listen at home. We want them to come out and hear her."

"Gotcha, buddy. Now I gotta run in the worst way. Later, tomcat."

"I don't know," said Olympia Clumpett, looking at her husband. "I do support the fire engine fund drive, of course. What do you think, Bucky? Should we agree to handle ticket sales today?"

"No, siree," said Bucky Clumpett. "We got a store to run, Limpy. But if the kids want to set up a card table over here by the orthopedic work boots and the tractor replacement parts, I guess we won't stop them. Make yourselves a sign, kids, and make yourselves at home."

Fawn, Stan, and Mike began to staff the card table, though until Ernie Latucci began to announce the special event, they sold only one ticket. That was to Old Man Fingerpie, who thought he was buying a book of matches and was annoyed when he couldn't light his pipe with the ticket. "I get in such a muddle!" he complained. Flossie Fingerpie clucked at him nicely and stuck his pipe between her own teeth lighting it and drawing a few breaths to get it going before handing it back to him.

"Decoration subcommittee," said Hector Yellow. He marched up and down the aisles of the Congregational/Unitarian church. There was nothing he could do about the red velvet seat cushions or the cracked plaster near the cornices over the windows. But he'd work with what he had.

"We want the décor to say: Spring," he proclaimed loudly. "It'll say: New life! It'll say: Fresh starts! It'll say: Music heals! It'll say: Feel the pulse! I want flowers, people, flowers from the hills and dales, irises if you can find them, dandelions if you must. I want ferns here, and here, and maybe over here?—too much?—no, no such thing as too much. I want a sweep of blue cloth, pinned to the pulpit and running like so, to resemble a flowing stream. Petunia Whiner can enter walking over the stream, a miracle arriving to charm our hearts. You got that, people?"

He was talking to himself. He was a subcommittee of one. Nobody else wanted to be on the decoration subcommittee.

"There's the problem of a backup band," said Mrs. Mildred Tweed, a.k.a. Petunia Whiner.

"Jasper Stripe, our janitor, plays the banjo," said Lois Kennedy the Third.

"And Grandma Earth plays the organ at penance services at Saint Mary," said Anna Maria.

"Shh," said Carly. When Grandma Earth played the organ, it was a penance service indeed. Grandma Earth was almost as devoid of musical skill as her daughter.

"Banjo, organ," mused Mrs. Tweed. "We need percussion. We need a rhythm section."

"Didn't Old Man Fingerpie play the snare drum during the Civil War?" asked Lois Kennedy the Third. But that was just a joke.

"We'll have to figure it out," said Mrs. Tweed. "Country music doesn't work without a good rhythm section. I'll require the backup players onstage by four so we can run through a few numbers." She was rummaging through her closets as she spoke. "All my standard country-western outfits, with the sequins and the braid and the epaulets and all—they're all in storage in a warehouse in Nashville. How vexing. And so are my hairpieces. I so wanted to go undercover in deepest Vermont. To live life out of the limelight for a change. But time marches on, and so must I. For the good of my son if not for myself. And the fire engine, too, of course."

"Well," said Fawn Petros, "my mom runs the Hamlet House of Beauty. And we can put our hands on a couple of wigs we know pretty well." She was thinking of the mounds of fake hair that had once served as Six Haunted Hairdos. Maybe with a little hairspray, they could make Mrs. Tweed look more like glamorous Petunia Whiner. She called up her mom's shop.

"Tell her to come over right away," said Fawn's mother on the phone. "I got Hank McManus here today because it's Saturday. The joint is hopping. Everyone's coming in to get their hair done for the benefit concert tonight. Your plan must be working, kids!"

Mrs. Tweed went rushing downstairs, hustled into her limo by Harold, her chauffeur. "But it's so tiresome," she was saying. "I haven't had time to audition for backup singers and dancers. I never go onstage without the Whine-ettes, and they're all in Bulgaria on a cultural exchange mission. The rush of this all—it makes me quite cross. I do hope I'll be up to giving a decent performance. Because when it's done right, there really is no business like show business. It's very rewarding indeed."

Professor Einfinger went into Grandma's Baked Goods and Auto Repair Shop. He bought a dozen jelly doughnuts from Grandma and asked her where her daughter was. "I think she's helping the mayor paint the auditorium at the high school today," she said. "You could go over there and find her."

That's exactly what he did. Miss Earth put down her roller and listened to his question. "Why, yes, I ride a motorcycle," she said. Then she remembered that Trooper Crawdad had talked about Geneworks agents showing up hunting for the chicks. Miss Earth didn't want to lie. But, like her students, she wanted to avoid telling all the truth she knew.

She didn't want to put the chicks at risk.

Cautiously, she said, "I've heard talk of a motorcycle hit by lightning here in town. Yes, I have. But I think you'll have to talk to Vermont State Trooper Hiram Crawdad for more particulars. That's all I have to say on the subject."

"I suppose I could stop at that general store in the center of town. I could nose around," said Einfinger. "Country stores are a dandy spot to pick up the local news." He noticed the pretty young teacher flinch at the words *general store*. Hmm, he said to himself. Check it out.

23. And a One, and a Two . . .

Ernie Latucci did his job. He wasn't called the Squawk of Vermont for nothing. By the time State Trooper Hiram Crawdad heard the news that Petunia Whiner was giving a surprise benefit concert at the Congregational/Unitarian church in Hamlet, Vermont, and called Clumpett's General Store to reserve a seat, he learned that all the tickets were sold out.

"But they can't be!" cried Trooper Crawdad. "I'm her biggest fan!"

"You and the rest of the world," sighed Limpy Clumpett. "Sales have gone through the roof. Every Bob and Bobcat is coming down out of the hills for this one. Look, Hiram, I can't talk to you now. I've got people three deep at the cash register weeping for tickets. All I can say is, hang around outside, and if there's a no-show, I'll get you in somehow." She corrected herself. "I mean, the kids will get you in if they can. It's their game." She handed the phone over to Mike Saint Michael, who was in charge of sales.

● ● ●

The children knew enough to hang back.

Mrs. Tweed was doing a quick dress rehearsal and sound check. She handed the charts on her latest compositions to the band. It was an odd-looking group of people. Jasper Stripe on banjo. Grandma Earth on the very churchy-sounding church organ. Father Fogarty held a triangle and the little metal stick with which to strike it. Mr. Bannerjee had shown up with a sitar and arranged himself on the Oriental carpet, propped up with some pillows. Then, just as Mrs. Tweed was announcing how vexing to be minus a rhythm section, in clumped Nurse Pinky Crisp. She was hauling two snare drums, a bass drum, a set of high hats, a cymbal, and four sets of drumsticks, in case she broke three of them in musical high spirits.

"Haven't played since the hospital jazz band," said Nurse Crisp, "but you never forget how to jam!"

"I do think I require backup vocals," said Mrs. Tweed.

"What do you suggest?" asked Father Fogarty. "It's a bit late to engage the Upper Valley Ecumenical Choir."

"I suppose it'll have to be the kids," said Mrs. Tweed. "A bit obvious, perhaps, but there you are. After all, why should I do all the hard work? Come on, you lot. I want each and every one of you up here, and we'll take it from the top."

"I can't sing!" sputtered Sammy Grubb. "I'm the Chief of the Copycats! It's not dignified!"

"I won't go on unless you do," said Mrs. Tweed. She crossed her arms. They had no choice.

Miss Earth left the high-school auditorium and rode her motorcycle over to Clumpett's to buy some soda for the volunteers doing the painting. As she parked in front of the store and dismounted, she noticed a car pulling up behind her. That Einfinger fellow had followed her! Right to the nest of the chicks! Rushing in, Miss Earth said to Mrs. Clumpett, "Olympia, someone's following me! I bet it's about those chickies! Get the alert out to some of the kids— I'll try to throw him off the scent!"

She hurried out of the store without stopping for her soda. She looked in the opposite direction from where Einfinger lingered and called stagily over her shoulder, "Thanks, Olympia! I'll deliver this seed to the chickies right away!"

What a bald-faced lie, she thought, reddening. I'm no better than Thud Tweed or his mother! I'm sure glad none of my students is here to witness it!

Then she hopped on her Kawasaki 8000 Silver Eagle and headed out of town, leading Professor Einfinger on a merry chase for the rest of the day. She had not realized until now that Professor Einfinger had assumed all the chicks had died. Miss Earth had given away the secret of the survival of at least some of them.

By seven-thirty the house was full. Even Trooper Crawdad had managed to squeeze in.

Almost all of Hamlet was there, as well as folks from neighboring Chumptown Falls, Forbush Corners, Sharon, Strafford, and Thetford. People called out greetings to each other across the room. The Reverend Mrs. Mopp had never witnessed such a crowd in her church. She wondered if she should take up country-western hymn singing to swell her congregation.

Miss Earth took her seat in the front row next to Mayor Grass.

"You never came back with the soda," he said.

"I had a busy afternoon," she answered. "I had a tailgater following me. But I think I lost him on the old muddy logging road over Hardscrabble Hill." She added, "This had better be good. So many folks paying ten dollars a head to get through the door!"

Mayor Grass did a quick head count—a professional skill he had developed in his capacity as occasional volunteer fireman. "I'd say three hundred, maybe three hundred and twelve," he said.

"At ten bucks a pop, best case scenario, that's three thousand dollars or more," said Miss Earth. "Back out a little donation to the church to cover electric bills, and they'll still clear twenty-seven hundred."

At twenty minutes to eight, the crowd started to get rowdy. They shouted and stamped on the floor.

At five minutes to eight, the noise of the crowd began to swell so mightily that the spring tree frogs down in Foggy Hollow thought a thunderstorm was on its way and croaked for joy.

Driving back into town, his car and his clothes covered with mud all over again, Wolfgang Einfinger heard the noise and thought, "Thunderstorm? Not again." He was amazed to see every inch of roadside crowded with cars. He had to drive almost as far as the Josiah Fawcett Elementary School and park there, then walk back to the green. What was going on here?

CLOSED, said the sign on Clumpett's General Store.

Good, thought Wolfgang Einfinger. Stuck in the muck

again on Hardscrabble Hill, he had had plenty of time to review what had happened today. That teacher and her tricks! He made an educated guess about where the chicks might be. Very educated. He tiptoed around the alley toward the Hen Hotel in the backyard of Clumpett's.

"Pe-Toon-YAH! Toon-YAH! Toon-YAAAAH!" brayed the audience, and then the houselights went down.

The crowd was silenced. Old Man Fingerpie could be heard, saying, "Flossie, did I drop my spectacles? Or do I even wear spectacles? I get in such a muddle!"

Then a spotlight swept down from the choir loft. "And now, ladies and gentleman," said the reverential, amplified voice of Ernie Latucci from somewhere in the back, "the Memphis Miracle, the Heart and Soul of Country-Western Music herself, the one, the only . . . Petunia Whiner!"

In the shadows, Mrs. Mildred Tweed murmured to herself, "Buck up, old girl, and do right by your only child."

Mrs. Tweed was left behind in the shadows. It was Petunia Whiner who stepped into the circle of light.

The crowd went wild. Petunia swept off her cowboy hat. Her copper thunderhead of a wig was magnificent enough to deserve an ovation all for itself. "Toon-YAH! Toon-YAH!" wailed the crowd in delirious thrill.

"Aww, tune yerself!" she answered, laughing. She flung her microphone eight feet in the air, twirled around, did a high kick as good as any nine-year-old Olympic gymnast could do, caught her microphone, and roared into it: "And a one, and a two . . . Well, awmighty heck, you're grownups! Count for yerselves!"

Professor Wolfgang Einfinger heard the roar of the audience as it screamed "Toon-Yah! Toon-Yah!" But he didn't give squat for country-western music. His mind was on finding the chicks. He brandished a flashlight, slicing a thin round of light in the bushes by the side of Clumpett's General Store, looking for the Hen Hotel.

"Why should my life be so hard?" he muttered to himself. "All I want is to find those little lizard-chicks and see what makes them tick. When Doctor Elderthumb hears some of them survived, I'll be rehabilitated in her eyes! Just let me scoop up the little nasties and get them over to Dartmouth. Let the specialist there do some delicate brain surgery. Skin the little scalp, pull back the little membrane, poke around a little bit and take some little notes. If the chick should die on the operating table, well, it's all in the name of science. The dead tissue will still give us lots of clues about how to provoke reverse evolution."

Professor Wolfgang Einfinger saw the Hen Hotel. He aimed the flashlight at the front door. Just as Petunia Whiner was making her appearance across the street in her spotlight, Doozy Dorking, at the door of the Hen Hotel, made her entrance into the spotlight of the flashlight. It made Professor Einfinger feel a bit odd. It was as if some imaginary crowd were going wild to see Doozy.

Doozy Dorking was in a fighting mood.

An hour or two ago, she'd been enjoying a sip of water from the bowl. When her back was turned, those kids had taken away her little chicks. She didn't like it. She didn't like it at all.

Maybe she heard Professor Einfinger murmur, "If the chicks should die . . . " and maybe she didn't. Anyway, she wasn't a murderess. But she didn't want to be granting interviews to some maddening scientist when her chicks were missing. She didn't have the time.

Doozy Dorking gave a mighty cluck and went on the attack.

Professor Wolfgang Einfinger was not having a good week.

He raised his hands to protect his face. The flashlight flew out of his hands and into the ceramic bowl of drinking water. The batteries lasted for a minute or so before the water got to them. A wavering light rippled around the hen yard as, with beak and claw, Doozy Dorking made known her opinion of intruders.

Over the green at the Congregational/Unitarian church, Petunia Whiner had the crowd eating out of her hand.

She'd done a string of hits one after the other. Then Mr. Dewey, the librarian, almost fainted when she called him up onstage to sing a duet with her, "The Overdue Library Book Blues." Petunia Whiner gave the nod to Nurse Pinky Crisp to go to town with the bass drum.

"*The judge bangs his hammer.* (SLAM! SLAM! went Nurse Pinky Crisp.)

Mah man's gotta go. (SLAM! SLAM!)
Spend time in the slammer (SLAM! SLAM!)
For hoardin' his dough. (SLAM! SLAM!)
And he'll read all the books they got in the prison
    LI-BRAIR-EE.
And he'll learn to behave, get out early, and quickly reTURN
    TO ME.
And he'll nevah nevah nevah (SLAM!)

Fail to pay
  His library fines again."

Petunia Whiner rolled her hips and thumbed through the pages of an imaginary book. Mr. Dewey pretended to stamp out and carry huge piles of books to show her. Nurse Pinky Crisp put a foot through her drum but kept on going.

After Mr. Dewey went back to his seat, Forest Eugene, working the panel, brought the stage lights down even lower. Petunia Whiner perched on a stool and put her elbows on her knees. She lowered her voice and said, "Let's have us a little one-on-one, cozy-like, shall we?"

Everyone hooted and whistled.

Petunia calmed them down. For a moment her speaking voice became a little bit Mildred Tweed. "To be serious, friends. I came to Vermont hoping to stay incognito. To nurse my wounds in private, to help protect my son from gossip columnists and paparazzi. I took a break from touring, but I fell into a pit of self-obsession. And my young man needed not just my presence but my attention. Now he has made friends for about the first time in his life. For that, a mother thanks you."

Everyone twitched uneasily. Vermonters tend to hate this kind of thing. Mrs. Tweed, a seasoned performing artist, sensed the change in the air and put a bit more Petunia into her voice. "You good folks in Hamlet taught him somethin' about loyalty and friendship. And ya've taught me, too. We've gotta stand by each other. Face the sorry facts o' life! Tell the truth and keep on cuddlin'!

"Now, folks, it's one thing to make a mistake. We all make mistakes. It's quite another ta admit it and have the courage ta make amends. Takes a heart bigger than mah hair ta do that. And these kids who thought up this fundraiser got heart. Ain't these kids got heart? Ain't it the truth? Ah'm asking ya!"

The crowd went wild again. The kids in Miss Earth's class all had to take a bow.

"And now, before we send you home with a smile in your heart and a song on your lips—"

"And a hole in our wallets!" called Mayor Grass, making everyone roar with laughter, including Petunia Whiner.

"—we got one last number to do. Now, folks. Let me introduce the band before we all disband. On the organ, Sassifying Sybilla Earth!"

Grandma Earth nodded to the applause. She began to noodle on the top notes, coaxing a whispery obliggato from the higher registers, like a piccolo with asthma.

"Oh, gosh," said Miss Earth, "it's her biggest hit ever— 'Stick with Your Man'!"

"Banjomeister Jasper Stripe!" said Petunia Whiner. Jasper Stripe huddled over his banjo and jazzily bent a few notes on it as if he were a rock star playing the Hollywood Bowl.

"After you, Father Fogarty!" said Petunia Whiner, and Father Fogarty began a syncopated rhythm on the triangle.

"The Guru of the Ganges, the Sage of the Sitar, Mr. Vandrishthatmatu Bannerjee!"

Mr. Bannerjee set up the ethereal drone on which the universe was founded, and this number as well.

"Feed a cold, starve a fever, but don't mess around with drum majorette Pinkella Crisp, R.N.!" said Petunia Whiner. Nurse Pinky Crisp tossed her drumsticks in the air and caught one with her left hand and the other with her teeth, without missing a beat or chipping a tooth.

"My backup chorus!" cried Petunia Whiner. The sixteen kids of Miss Earth's class—Copycats, Tattletales, Rotten Egg, and Pearl Hotchkiss—began to hum on several notes that didn't exactly match, but the crowd was howling so appreciatively that nobody noticed.

"A-one! A-two!"

"STOPPPP!" cried a voice.

There was the briefest of pauses. Everyone turned. At the back door stood Professor Wolfgang Einfinger. There was blood on his face. Was it his or Doozy Dorking's? "I WANT THOSE CHICKS!" he shouted. "WHERE ARE THEY?"

Trooper Crawdad was at Professor Einfinger's side in an instant. "Don't make a public nuisance," he said. "The show must go on."

"A-one two three!" yelled Petunia Whiner.

Then it began. "Stick with Your Man." The most rocking, rolling, foot-stamping, hand-clapping version ever of Petunia Whiner's biggest Number One Hit. It had been a runaway crossover on the charts. It had won the Grammy for Best Song and the Oscar for Best Song and the Pulitzer Prize for Best Song. But it had never been given a treatment like this, and it never would again.

> *"Blizzards snow, tornadoes blow.*
> *Ingrown toenails come and go.*
> *Troubles grow, but even so,*
> *Girl, here's what you gotta know:"*

Everyone in the room sang the famous last line:

> *"Stick with your man!"*

Then there was a surprise guest appearance. To be more precise, three of them.

● ● ●

Backstage, the three little chicks had gone crazy with all the noise. At Olympia Clumpett's suggestion, Amos, Beatrice, and Seymour had been spirited away from Doozy Dorking and the Hen Hotel by their minders. There was too much to do at the church, getting ready for the concert, to find another hiding place. Besides, what better hiding place for genetically altered chicks than backstage at a church?

But the clapping and foot stamping as one hit number followed another had dislodged the makeshift pen that the former Rotten Eggs had built for the chicks in the Reverend Mrs. Mopp's study. For an hour or more the three chicks had been on the loose in the back rooms of the vestry. Finally, just as Petunia Whiner had wound up the concert with her biggest hit of all time, the chicks had bumped through the half-open door at the side of the church hall, and the lights and noise and uplifting sound of music had drawn them into the fold.

The three little chicks wandered into the limelight. However savage their gene combinations, they were soothed by music. In fact, they were busy kicking and preening in time. They strutted their little fuzzy stuff. They were naturals. The crowd went wild.

Petunia Whiner didn't see them for a second. She just launched into the second verse.

> *"Earthquakes shake, fires bake,*
> *Every waking heart can break.*
> *Don't you make a big mistake.*
> *Girl, come on, for goodness' sake:*
> *Stick with your man!"*

Then Petunia Whiner did a twirl and saw the three chicks. They did a twirl, too. They were very talented. Petunia did a little hop, and they hopped, too.

Petunia Whiner interjected in the bridge, "Let's give it up for Soul Poultry!" The crowd went even wilder. The Flameburpers managed a syncopated little cakewalk while emitting tiny blats of flame on the off beat.

"They're everything we hoped for and more!" yelled Professor Wolfgang Einfinger above the crowd. "They're the first step in reverse evolution! Let me at 'em!" He broke free from Trooper Crawdad and began to claw his way through the room toward the stage.

> *"Showers pour, hurricanes roar,*
> *Your hairdo looks like it's been in a war.*
> *Pimples make your skin so sore.*
> *But girl, remember what you're for:*
> *Stick with your man!"*

The crowd was so excited, they didn't realize who Professor Wolfgang Einfinger was after. They thought he was some crazed fan who wanted to be near Petunia Whiner. But Thud saw what was coming. He shouted to his mother. "Mom!" he said. "Trouble! Mix it up!"

Petunia Whiner didn't know what Thud was talking about, but she was first and foremost a pro. "Encore: 'Burping,' double time!" she whispered to her backup band, which by now was functioning with lazy precision as if they'd been together for decades. They launched into a stepped-up version of "Baby Needs Burping."

Petunia started to clap her hands over her head. The crowd was already on its feet after the standing ovation it had given "Stick with Your Man." Petunia leaped off the stage area into the middle of the audience.

"Stop them! Seize them!" yelled Professor Einfinger. Salim, Lois, and Thud grabbed the Flameburpers and hustled them off the stage toward the side door. But the crowd was too revved up to pay attention to one more nut going gaga over Petunia Whiner. So under cover of rapturous ovations, all of Miss Earth's students escorted the three cloned chicks out into the night.

24. Lightning Strikes Twice

With all the hoopla inside the church building, no one had heard the distant thunder. But a storm was sweeping up the Connecticut River Valley from central Massachusetts. Lilac bushes rustled their tender new leaves. Hard rain rattled fitfully against the side of the church. Somewhere to the south, thunder rumbled. Lightning backlit the Green Mountains around Hamlet. High spring weather, in all its glory.

"Where should we go?" shouted Sammy.

"Back to the Hen Hotel," answered Thekla. "That madman must've been a Geneworks scientist! And I think he's not just mad, he's *mad*. What if he's hurt Doozy Dorking?"

The thought was too horrible to contemplate. The children ran even faster. The chicks were scared of the commotion, of the wind and rain. They didn't like being out at night. They peeped in little frightened burps. "Ow," said Thud. "Watch that flameburping, Amos."

They hurried across the green. The town was quiet, with three quarters of the population packed into the building across the street. Clumpett's looked sad and still, like the stage set for a movie. The only light inside glowed coldly from the stand-up coolers, yellowed by the reflection off gilt-lettered beer cans.

"Don't look now," said Anna Maria. They all looked. Professor Wolfgang Einfinger had broken free of Trooper Crawdad and was wheeling across the road toward them. They all shrieked and put on the steam. "Scatter!" shouted Sammy Grubb. As the rain broke, the kids peeled off in different directions. Professor Einfinger paused, not knowing which of the children had the chicks. But Thud ran around one side of Clumpett's General Store, and Lois and Salim hustled themselves around the other side. They met at the front door of the Hen Hotel.

Doozy Dorking was lying prostrate on the Hen Hotel's little fretted ramp. Was she dead, or merely fainted into a hennish coma? "Doozy," cried Lois. "Wake up! We have your little chicks back!" The children placed the chicks on the ground near Doozy, to be encouraging to her.

Doozy dozed, or decomposed, one or the other. It was hard to tell.

"Doozy!" said Thud. He stroked the hen's forehead. "Did that freaky scientist kill you? Come back to life! Your chicks need you!"

Salim and Lois leaned over to see. Could you do CPR on a hen?

Two of the chicks on the ground began to twitter and jump and burp protesting flames. "What? What is it?" said Salim, and turned around. "Oh, no," he said.

Professor Einfinger had the third chick in his hands. It looked like Seymour.

"Put him down," said Salim.

"Give me the others," said Professor Einfinger. "They're mine."

"They're not yours," said Lois. "That's chicken slavery. They belong to themselves. Put him down."

Seymour was a pacifist. Alone of the chicks, he had never burped flame at a living creature. He didn't know how, even as Professor Einfinger's hands closed tightly around him.

"Give me the other two," said Professor Einfinger, "or I'll wring this one's neck. And when I'm done with that, I'll wring yours."

"AAAAAAGH!" screamed Thud suddenly, like a bellowing gorilla, and he was up off his knees and rushing for Professor Einfinger so fast that no one had seen it coming. Thud lowered his head and *became* his name. One huge unstoppable THUD. He thudded into Professor Einfinger's belly. Seymour flew up in the air, released like a little fuzzy yellow tennis ball, and fell to the ground, unhurt. Thud pummeled Professor Einfinger with his fists. Lois and Salim screamed for help. But who could hear them? Only the Copycats and Tattletales and Pearl Hotchkiss, since Petunia Whiner seemed to be leading the rest of the town in a rendition of "The Battle Hymn of the Republic."

Amos the Flameburper danced closer, jumping up and down excitedly, trying to apply little licks of flame to Professor Einfinger's kicking feet.

"Stop!" cried Lois. "Violence never solved anything!"

"Try nonviolent resistance!" cried Salim. "Thud, stop!"

But what stopped Thud wasn't the objections of his friends. It was lightning. With a crackling sound, a fire bolt unbuckled itself from the thunderclouds and sliced itself to the earth, like the terrible swift sword in the song. The nighttime world went into black-and-white reverse: The clouds turned white, the air turned black. One prong of the lightning struck a transformer on the edge of town, knocking out the power grid that fed Hamlet. The town and everything in it plunged into primordial darkness.

But the other prong struck a tree in the forest on the hill behind Clumpett's General Store. The surge traveled through the soil in seven zillionths of an instant, throwing up dirt and leaves as it burrowed. It struck the Hen Hotel with two consequences.

The happy one was that it must have provided the needed electrochemical jolt to start Doozy Dorking's heart again. She sat up like a chicken fond of aerobic exercise and threw back her head and clucked with a huge thunderlike roar.

"CLUUUUUUUUUUUUUUUUUUUUUCK!"

The unhappy consequence was that the power also ran up the walls of the Hen Hotel behind her. All four walls and the ceiling of the icehouse burst into flames. Doozy took one look at the inferno and lit out for safer territory. At the rate she was going, she seemed likely to hit Ohio before she paused for breath.

The kids screamed. It had all happened so fast! The power was off, the Hen Hotel had been torched, Professor Einfinger was rolling to his feet, Doozy Dorking was alive and well—though outta here in a big way—

—and Seymour the Flameburper was dead.

"No," said Salim. "No. No."

But it was true. Seymour lay on his side, a few drops of

blood leaking through his eye sockets. The front of his little chest was burned, a scorching brown vest of chicken fuzz. Amos was hovering over him.

"Amos!" cried Lois. "Did you do that?"

Amos the Flameburper turned. He had a strange expression on his face. He looked at Thud as if expecting to be praised. Thud, who had rolled off Professor Einfinger, was sitting on the muddy ground, horrified.

"I didn't do that," said Professor Einfinger. "However, the chick does look dead. So I'll take its carcass and perform some tests on it—"

He couldn't finish his sentence. From around one corner of the store came Thekla Mustard and the Tattletales. Around the other corner rushed Sammy Grubb and the Copycats. They threw themselves onto Professor Einfinger in a kind of scrimmage pileup.

Pearl Hotchkiss wasn't there. She was running back to the church to sound the fire alarm. An ember from the roof of the Hen Hotel had leaped to the roof of Clumpett's General Store. If the store caught fire and the flames traversed the roof beam, the gas tanks in the front of the store would blow. It would mean the end of Hamlet, Vermont, and all its inhabitants. Schoolchildren across Vermont would have to cross the name of Hamlet off the map.

25. The Good Egg?

If Clumpett's General Store had caught on fire any other night that spring, it wasn't likely that the fire could have been contained. With only a single working fire engine, the town of Hamlet was at great risk for fire damage. But this one night alone, almost everyone in town was present at the Petunia Whiner benefit gala. Therefore, it was the work of but a moment for everyone to rush across the green to help. Fire Chief Lester Cobble organized a bucket brigade. Prompt work insured that the smoking roof of Clumpett's didn't erupt into a firestorm. After a while, engines from the surrounding towns showed up with their hoses. That the rain kept coming down heavier and heavier was a big help, too.

Though Thud was well known as a liar, Salim and Lois, through their tears, backed his statements up. So Trooper Crawdad slapped handcuffs on Wolfgang Einfinger. The state trooper arrested the professor for threatening one Master Thaddeus Nero Tweed, a minor, with assault and battery. "With a temper like that, you think I'm going to release those little chicks into your custody?" said Trooper Crawdad. "No way. Maybe they're Geneworks chicks, maybe not. For the time being, they're wards of the state of Vermont. We'll let the courts decide."

"You maniac!" shouted Einfinger.

"And furthermore, I changed my mind about that speeding ticket," said Trooper Hiram Crawdad. "I'm going to slap you with a big fat fine. So there."

Many townspeople wept at the sight of the little body of Seymour the Flameburper. True Vermonters, they were glad that their tears were camouflaged as raindrops.

"I'll take care of the little critter," said Mayor Grass. "I'll bury him in some secret spot on town property. I won't mark the grave, to keep spying scientists from digging him up. Leave it to me. The poor little Flameburper."

Salim put his hands over Seymour's cold body for one last time.

Then he got into his car between his father and his mother and he went home.

He was too upset to notice what Thud and Lois noticed.

The two Flameburpers left were Beatrice and Amos. But in the fuss over trying to save Clumpett's General Store, the two little chicks had been hustled aside under an upturned plastic milk crate at the far end of Clumpett's backyard.

And one of the chicks had flamed its way through the plastic, melting a little gateway in it. When Lois and Thud went to retrieve Beatrice and Amos, one of them was gone. It had broken out of its prison and escaped into the woods near Foggy Hollow.

But neither Lois nor Thud could tell which chick had escaped.

For several days now they hadn't needed the colored yarns to tell the chicks apart. Amos had been feisty and athletic, the strongest and most aggressive of them. Beatrice had been a bit smaller, more chirpy, good-natured, more affectionate. Seymour had seemed serious, even serene. Though created from roughly the same material, Flameburpers A, B, and C had already turned into themselves, with tiny, discreet personalities.

But the chick who was left: Was it Amos or Beatrice? Without picking it up to check, they couldn't tell. It wasn't behaving like either one of them. It didn't blat out any flames or waggle its bum. Its little green sprig of feathers up top was flopped over, listless.

Was the chick just suffering from shock and grief? Or was the last remaining Flameburper in captivity going through some sort of metamorphosis? Was it turning into something larger than, or later than, or newer than, or more reverse than, or just plain *other* than the Amos or the Beatrice it had once been? Was this Amos Version Two Point 0? Was this Beatrice the Second?

Thud and Lois gave the chick to Flossie Fingerpie, who agreed to take it home and let Lot's Wife, the last remaining hen, take it under her wing. If she would. Old Man Fingerpie didn't care. He was asleep in the car. He'd slept through most of Petunia Whiner's concert and all the raging of fire-engine sirens coming through Hamlet.

The next day was Sunday.

At the Congregational/Unitarian church, the Reverend

Mrs. Mopp gave a sermon called "Ringing Fire Alarms and Singing Fiery Hymns." It was a humdinger. Nurse Pinky Crisp's drum ensemble was still set up in the vestry, lending a sort of atmosphere to her remarks.

At Saint Mary in the Tombstones, Father Fogarty thanked all his parishioners who had rolled up their shirtsleeves and helped save the general store. "Clumpett's is as much a center of town life as the schools, the churches, and the library," he said. "Let us pray in gratitude that it was spared."

On Sunday afternoon, Lois Kennedy the Third got on her bike and rode over to the old Munning estate. When she got to the front door, she rang the bell. She stood there for a long time. Finally the door was opened. Mrs. Tweed looked out. In one hand she carried a tea cup, and with the other hand she clutched her gray silk moiré bathrobe closed against her throat.

"It's Lois, I see," she said. "Good morning. How do you do?"

"Fine. You were great last night," said Lois. "Thanks a lot. Is Thud home?"

"Out back," said Mrs. Tweed. "And Lois? Thank you for inviting me to sing. I did it for Thaddeus as well as for the town. It was about time."

"You're welcome," said Lois. "Are you going to keep living here now that your cover is blown?"

"I can't say at the moment," said Mrs. Tweed. "I'm trying not to make rash decisions." She closed the door gently.

Lois rode the bike around the corner of the house and found Thud lying on a stone bench. His eyes were closed, and he looked lonely.

When he heard her approaching, he opened his eyes. They were wet. "What are you doing here, you busybody?" he said nastily. He sat up and blew his nose.

"Come on," said Lois. "Let's get going."

"I'm not going anywhere," said Thud.

"Oh, yes you are," said Lois. "We're going to see Salim."

"Why?" said Thud.

"I don't have to tell you. I think you know," said Lois. "You might be the last remaining Rotten Egg, but you're still the Boss. You know what we have to do. Don't you?"

"I don't do anything for anyone," he said. "I never have and I never will."

"Thud," said Lois, "you're a pretty good liar. We've learned that. But you're lying again. You *do* do things for people. In your own mean, cranky way, you made a small club for me and Salim when we were divorced from our own clubs. Maybe you didn't mean to be kind, but you were. Even with a name like Thud, you couldn't help it."

There was a silence. The boy looked away. "I guess you're right," said Thud at last. "Come on. Let's go to the Bannerjees' house."

Salim's face was thin and drawn, and his eyes huge and raw from crying. But when they told him what had happened to the other two Flameburpers, he pulled himself together. "May I go out?" he asked his parents.

"Of course, go out with your little friends," said Mrs. Bannerjee. Mr. Bannerjee couldn't speak. He was lying on the sofa with a hot-water bottle on his forehead. For his experience doing backup sitar for Petunia Whiner he required some time for recovery.

The kids rode their bikes over to Old Man Fingerpie's farm on Squished Toad Road. Flossie Fingerpie was making flapjacks. "I've been too tired after last night to go take a look-see," she said to them. "You go have a gander at the little critter and tell me about it. I know at the age of ninety-six I'm a spring chick compared to Old Man Fingerpie, but I still feel the decades in my bones, of a morning."

They wandered around to Old Man Fingerpie's barn. It was nice to see it full again, occupied by the animals that had been housed elsewhere while the Fingerpies were in Florida. A cat licking itself in the sunlight. A pig that smelled like a pig. A couple of geese already out on the cold pond, resembling two large cake ornaments made of glistening spun sugar. And there was Lot's Wife, standing still and paying no attention to anything at all.

"Not a great choice for a stepparent," said Lois. "A catatonic chicken."

But they heard a familiar voice. A cluck of welcome. Out of the shadows of the barn into the sunlight strutted Doozy Dorking, followed by Amos or Beatrice, whichever it was.

"Doozy!" cried Thud. "You've come home to roost!"

Doozy proudly observed her adopted chick. The little yellow thing ran up to the former Three Rotten Eggs and jumped up and down as if excited to see them. Lois, Salim, and Thud knelt on the ground and looked at it closely to see if they could identify it.

They still couldn't tell if it was Amos or Beatrice. But they could tell that something new was happening to it.

Its little yellow peach fuzz coating was slightly browned.

Scorched? Self-scorched? It seemed to be coming loose. As the kids looked, more fluffy down frizzled up and dropped away.

The green crest of feathers up top had a slightly spikier, spinier look to it.

"No wonder we can't tell if it's Amos or Beatrice," said Lois. "It's changing into something different. Like . . . a butterfly crawling from the chrysalis of a caterpillar."

"Right. But is it a butterfly," asked Thud, "or a butt kicker?"

"Why do you say that?" said Lois.

"If this is Amos," said Thud, "I have to take the blame. I've been a liar and a cheat and a bully. I've been a bad example. Maybe I'm the reason Amos went bad. Maybe he attacked poor Seymour just to make himself feel big and strong. Thudlike."

"Maybe," said Lois. "But if this was Amos, he's turning into something else now. And so can you."

Salim spoke almost for the first time all day. "Besides," he said carefully, "we don't know for sure that Amos attacked Seymour. Maybe Seymour just died. The excitement. He was a very tender-hearted chick. Genetically altered creatures might be prone to early collapse. Amos shouldn't take the rap if we don't have proof. A chick is innocent until proven guilty."

Thud said, "We'll never know."

"No," said Lois, "I guess we won't. All we can ever be really sure of is that *we're* not finished changing yet, either. There's still more to go, and it's up to us which way it goes."

They sat there in the sun, watching the chick.

It worked with zeal and energy, as if eager to change itself into something new. However strange a creature, its genes tinkered with by scientists, then power-surged by a freak lightning bolt, it was doing its best to become itself. Maybe the first of its kind ever in the universe.

And it was spring, when new creatures emerge. The sun dappled the barnyard. High in the white pines, a few blue jays called. Doozy Dorking looked up from pecking the ground to watch her stepchild begin to grow up. Would it be bad or good? Did Doozy Dorking have sharp motherly instincts? Could she tell? Who knew what she thought of the last remaining Flameburper?

The last remaining Flameburper in captivity, that is.

If it hadn't been eaten by foxes yet, another Flameburper was still out there somewhere. On the loose, all alone, lost in the wild.

Epilogue

Professor Wolfgang Einfinger was released on bail. He was told never to set foot within the town limits of Hamlet again. He disobeyed at once. It was but the work of a moment for him to find out that the last known chick had been billeted at Old Man Fingerpie's farm.

He showed up the next Saturday evening and knocked on the door. Flossie was washing her hair in the kitchen sink, so Old Man Fingerpie got himself out of his rocker and hobbled over.

He listened to Einfinger's blather about chicks and chickens. "Oh, I know who you mean," said Old Man Fingerpie. He went to the freezer and took out a plastic bag of frozen chicken. "The chick got big very fast. She went through a growth spurt like we never seen before. We were afraid she might explode. Something weird about that bird. But tasty. We wrung her neck and ate her. Here's what's left of her. You can take it and perform your experiments on her if you like. She was pretty tough to chew, especially if like me you don't have any teeth. She tasted like grilled gizzard, or loin of lizard, or boiled buzzard, or something."

Einfinger couldn't believe his good luck. Dr. Elderthumb would forgive him his ineptitude! They could subject this frozen chicken flesh to all manner of tests and find out the secrets of reverse evolution! They hadn't lost their chance to rule the world with cheap labor! Everything depended on what they learned from this sample. "Thank you," said Einfinger, and fled before someone younger and less out of it came along and recognized him.

Flossie Fingerpie emerged from the kitchen with her head wrapped in a towel.

"What were you telling that nosy stranger?" she asked her ancient husband. "You know perfectly well that the last little chick is still out there in the hen yard with Doozy Dorking, minding its own business. Did you just tell a lie to that scientific man? Did you just hand over the frozen carcass of Minerva? I was going to make a chicken pot pie for Sunday with the leftovers."

"Oh, I get in such a muddle," said Old Man Fingerpie. "It's terrible to be so old. I get so confused, I never know what I'm saying."

He grinned at her and went out to scatter some corn. There were some things he was never in a muddle about, and spring was one of them.

7.05